KV-108-009

KILLER STAR

by C T Furlong

an **arctic**6
adventure

INSIDE
POCKET

Also by C T Furlong

Killer Strangelets
Killer Genes

Tameside Libraries	
3 8016 0200 0002	
PETERS	23-Jun-2015
JF	£5.99
CEN	

TAMESIDE LIBRARIES

‖‖‖‖‖‖‖‖‖‖‖‖‖‖‖‖‖‖‖‖‖‖‖

3 8016 0200 00024

WITHDRAWN FROM
TAMESIDE LIBRARIES

KILLER
STAR

This is a work of fiction. Names, characters, places and
incidents are either the product of the author's imagination
or, if real, used fictitiously.

Published in Great Britain by
Inside Pocket Publishing Limited
First published in Great Britain in 2011

Text copyright © C T Furlong, 2011

The right of C T Furlong to be identified as the author of this
work has been asserted in accordance with the Copyright,
Designs and Patents Act 1988.

All rights reserved. No part of this publication may be
reproduced, stored in a retrieval system or transmitted in any
form or by any means, electronic, mechanical, photocopying,
recording or otherwise, without the prior permission of
the publishers.

A CIP catalogue record for this book is available from
the British Library

ISBN 978-0-9562315-8-1

10 9 8 7 6 5 4 3 2

Inside Pocket Publishing Limited Reg. No. 06580097
Printed and bound in Great Britain by
CPI Bookmarque Ltd, Croydon

www.insidepocket.co.uk

Prologue

'Start recording me now, Charlie!'

'OK, Renny. Three, two, one... iPhone recording.'

'Hello, people. For those of you who don't know me, my name is Renny Johnson. All I ask is that you listen to the story we're about to tell you. Listen carefully to all sides. And then - well, you know the drill. Lines will open once we've finished. Please call to vote for who you think is right. You'll have ten minutes. Please don't call after the lines close as your vote won't count and you may still be charged. It's all down to you now. Here are the numbers you need to call. If you want to vote for Iago then call 555-1235 and add a 1, for Charlie - add a 2...'

'Renny!'

'*What*, Charlie?'

'What are you doing? This is serious, you know!'

'I *am* being serious. I think this format will work best. We don't know who's right and who's wrong, so I think we should let our audience guide us.'

'But this is way too important to put out to the public vote. This needs to be decided by people in charge. You know - elected representatives.'

'But we were recruited by elected representatives, Charl'. Well - not exactly *by* them, but by their people. Anyway, this isn't going out on normal channels. But I *will* broadcast over a few more mainstream networks.'

'What do you mean? Are you're talking about broadcasting on television?'

'No! That's dinosaur stuff. Only adults use normal television these days. I'm going to stream via gaming channels. Kids all over the world are hooked up. And don't worry - it's not just going out to the World of Warcrafters. I'm including all the world-building sites as well. But it has to be fair. OK? So I'll tell the whole story right up to this point. After that, you and Iago will both get your turn. Then, at the very least, we listen to what our people think.'

'They're not *our* people, Renny. You don't know them. They'll probably just respond to your survey to get rid of your little pop-up and go straight back to their shooting.'

'They've always helped us out in the past. We wouldn't have been able to activate Dad's failsafe without them. Killer Strangelets would have gobbled up the Earth if Katherina Kreng had managed to get control of the Large Hadron Collider. Only *their* phone calls turned that satellite around. All our heroics would've come to nothing without *those* people. And besides...'

'Besides *what*?'

'Well - they won't be able to ignore me. My friend

B-Punk can make sure that ours is the only gameplay available to them. We'll get their attention all right!'

Geekboss: need a game intercept

B-Punk: what game?

Geekboss: all of 'em

B-Punk: whaaaaaaaaaaaat?

Geekboss: well - many as you can.

B-Punk: serious????

Geekboss: deadly

B-Punk: 4 when?

Geekboss: now

B-Punk: lol

Geekboss: no lol. how soon?

B-Punk: dunno. send your signal. will stream when I can

Geekboss: livestreaming now

1

London
Wednesday 13th July

I get all kinds of communications from sources all round the world. Some of them can be pretty obscure - you might even say weird. But I've developed a nose for the truly strange. Anything hinky pings on my radar as soon as I sit at my desk.

It's usually nothing more than happy hackers or zealous followers trying to get my attention, but every now and then one of them makes me sit up straight and take a harder look.

ARCTIC6 have become well known in certain circles, although we try to keep a fairly low profile. After we helped save the President of the United States last year, he promised my cousin Iago that he'd do his best to keep us out of the news. In geekworld though, I'm pretty well known. I've had to reach out to so many of my geekfriends in the past that I can't cover it up. They all know me... I've even got a fan club.

Now, I'm not going to bore you with too much detail, but let's just say that this particular message came to me through a very unusual source. It wasn't a mail, tweet or in-game message. It was a malicious worm that set off all sorts of bells and whistles. Well - what I mean is that my antivirus programs went into overdrive. I had warnings flashing everywhere on my screen. I have a lot of protection packages, some of them unique and hand coded for me by the best white-hats out there. People say that I'm paranoid, but you can't be too careful!

Oh, for those of you who don't know, 'white-hats' are white-hat hackers. These are guys who used to be on the dark side, but have now gone over to the light. They're basically hackers who've been persuaded to work for the people they used to hack. They're security experts.

Imagine you're a big company and you want to make your network or data secure. What do you do? Well, you employ someone to try to hack your system to see where your weaknesses are. That person is a white-hat hacker.

Anyway, as you can imagine there are people out there who'd love to get into my system. My white-hats make sure that doesn't happen.

That's why, when this worm attacked, I was all ears. My protection packages are amongst *the* best in the world, so somebody serious was on to me.

I finally found their worm, chomping away merrily in a corner of my system. It looked so innocent there, as if it had just got itself lost. It didn't try to do anything when I probed it. It just gave itself up, which made me even more suspicious. These things don't usually just lie down and die.

I talked to my geeksquad about what I should do with it. Well - when I say talked; I mean we messaged each other on our computers. We never actually *talk* to each other!

These guys have helped me in the past. Their collective hive-mind is pretty powerful. They may be geeks, but when the chips were down, they helped the ARCTIC6 save the world from Killer Strangelets - and the rest, but that's a different story.

Eventually, the geeksquad got back to me. We decided that knowing was better than not, so we'd have a go at dissecting the worm. At first, it looked just like any other piece of malware...

Everything in the worm's code was what I'd expected to see, right up until the last line. My geeks were all tuned in so they could see what I could see. My Croatian uber-geek, Dragosh - not his real name - dropped in. I'd given him remote access to my network, just temporarily while I investigated the worm. I was worried things might get out of hand.

Dragosh turned the worm over, checking its belly for any codebombs or data-ticks. The rest of us were deadly quiet.

It wasn't that I couldn't rebuild my network. Between us, we were capable of rebuilding even the most complicated hub, but there would be irrecoverable data loss if anything went wrong.

I'd almost chewed my nail to the quick by the time he'd finished his check.

'What is it?' I asked his avatar: the image he uses to represent himself online - no one's ever actually seen Dragosh.

'It looks like - a tiny piece of firmware.'

His weird tinny voice echoed through my laptop speakers. Dragosh uses audio encryption to change his voice. Today he had the croaky voice of an old man.

'Do you think it's meant to unlock something?' I asked.

'Probably just some hacker trying to send you a message,' cut in Aaron, my West Coast contact.

'No!' replied Dragosh. 'This looks serious.'

'Should we let it run?' I asked.

'I can't extract it,' replied Dragosh, 'so either we try to kill it, or we take a chance.'

I thought about my systems, and how much I loved them, and how valuable all my programs were. But in the end, curiosity won out - I needed to know what would happen next.

'Run it,' I almost whispered.

Without a word, Dragosh did it. From the four corners of the globe, me and the rest of the geeksquad studied our screens.

'What's it doing?' Aaron asked.

'It looks like it's establishing a link,' said Dragosh.

'I can see it,' I said. 'It seems to be accessing my video-streaming device.'

My screen glitched and in that split-second both Dragosh and Aaron's avatars disappeared from view. In their place, on my screen, was the back-lit silhouette of someone sitting in a chair. Although this person was nowhere near me, my heart began pounding. Somehow, they'd managed to get into my systems and that made me more than a little nervous.

'Who... who are you?' I asked, swallowing hard.

'Don't worry, Renny, you're not in any danger,' the man replied.

His voice was silky and soft, but this man had just

hacked into my system. Besides, I couldn't even see his face, which made me trust him even less. And he knew my name. A small shiver snaked up my spine.

'Like I said - *who* are you?'

I narrowed my eyes as best I could, and clenched my jaw like I'd seen Iago do.

Without looking at it, I clicked the record icon on my desktop. It activated a camera on the shelf just above my left shoulder. This man, whoever he was, wasn't going to leave a copy of this message on my computer. The quality of my recording wouldn't be great but I'd be able to play it back to the others.

'Let's not bother with names for now - shall we? I'm sure you know that in this business, a name doesn't really mean anything.'

'Um - *what* business are you in?'

That didn't come out as steadily as I'd hoped.

'Let's just say that I work for the Government...'

'Which department?'

'None you will have heard of.'

'Are you a spy?'

'I work for the security services.'

'MI5? MI6?'

'They warned me you'd ask a lot of questions.'

'Stop changing the subject!' I shouted, though I wondered who'd warned him. This guy was as slippery as a wet mackerel.

'The department I represent,' he said, 'is a cousin of MI5 and MI6.'

'What's this cousin called then?'

'SOE.'

'SOE? You mean the Special Operations Executive?'

'Yes.'

'Come *on*. I may be a kid but even I know that was shut down shortly after the Second World War.'

History isn't my strongest subject, but secret organisations light up on my radar.

'Listen, Renny - you're right - technically the SOE hasn't existed for a very long time. After the war, all the agents involved in 'operations' against our enemies were either folded into MI5 or MI6. However, although the body was cut off, the head remained intact.'

'So there's still a department somewhere that plans operations against enemy targets? But - we're not at war any more!'

'There are always wars, Renny,' he replied.

I felt stupid. Of course, there were wars. And I suppose what he was saying made sense. You wouldn't really want to shut down a department like SOE. What if you needed to carry out covert operations on foreign soil?

'But,' I said, 'if you have no operatives... how do you carry out operations?'

'We usually use freelancers.'

His reply surprised me a bit. By *freelancers,* of course he meant mercenaries - people who did these kinds of things for profit.

'Um... listen, Mr whoever-you-are, this is all very interesting, but why are we having this conversation?'

'Because I need you, Renny.'

'Whhaaattttt?'

This had to be some kind of joke. One of my geeks was trying to set me up. I threw my hands up and laughed.

'All right - whoever's put you up to this, just tell 'em you got me. I've been pranked, or punked, or whatever!'

'Seriously, Renny, this isn't a job for some meathead for hire. This is a bit more sensitive than that. We need someone we can trust one hundred per cent.'

'And *we're* what you came up with?'

'ARCTIC6 is on everyone's radar - friend, or foe,' he said.

'What?'

Was I hearing things? Why would they want us? Of course, it wouldn't be difficult for someone with access to find out that the ARCTIC6 - Iago, Charlie, Cam, Tara, Aretha and I - had done some amazing things in the past. But we were still just kids.

'We need your special skillset and I'd like to meet you all,' he replied.

'Why didn't you just call us?' I asked.

'This needs to be completely and totally off the radar.'

'Off whose radar?'

'Everyone's...'

I didn't know what to say. I think I just sat there with my mouth open for a while. The man turned away from the window and faced the camera.

'We'll contact you again. But Renny... this time, please keep your geekfriends out of it. We only need the ARCTIC6!'

Then he was gone, and Aaron and Dragosh's avatars reappeared on the screen in front of me.

2

Well, I couldn't exactly tell Aaron and Dragosh what had happened, so I fobbed them off with some waffle about the virus taking out my video device. Aaron just nodded and said his goodbyes, but Dragosh's avatar stuck around a bit, staring at me. Dragosh had a fully animated avatar. He used something very similar to an Xbox Kinect to track his movements and relay them to the image on screen.

I could tell that he didn't believe me, and guilt crept up on me, making my hands fumble on the keyboard. Finally, his avatar just shrugged, muttering 'whatever', and vanished. I breathed out a huge sigh of relief.

I contacted the rest of the ARCTIC6 and got them together as quickly as I could.

'Do you think he's for real?' asked Aretha, after we'd all watched the recording through a few times.

'Sounds like one of your geeks having a laugh,' said Cam.

I looked up at him. He was smirking.

'If it was one of your nerdy friends,' said Tara, 'he's a pretty good actor.'

'I agree,' said Charlie. 'That really looked like an

adult. I didn't know your guys could do stuff like that. They should be working in Hollywood!'

My computer pinged.

'Incoming,' I shouted above the chatter, racing to my desk.

I looked up. As usual, nobody was paying attention.

'You guys!' I shouted.

Five pairs of eyes turned towards me. Well - six actually, if you counted Bandit's. That dog hadn't left Aretha's side since she'd adopted him after our last adventure.

The same image as earlier appeared on my screen. It seemed that the malicious worm had left a channel open. This man could drop in whenever he liked.

'Hello Iago,' came the silky tones of the silhouetted man, as my cousin leaned in over my shoulder.

'Who are you?' asked Iago without a second's hesitation.

'As I told Renny...'

Iago cut him off. 'We don't deal with nameless silhouettes!'

'Which is precisely why I wanted to arrange a meeting - face to face.'

The man's voice remained even-toned and smooth. Iago hadn't ruffled him at all.

'Why should we meet you?' Iago continued. 'What's this about?'

'Saving the planet,' the man answered.

'Is this some kind of a joke?' My cousin stood up straight now, glancing around at the rest of us.

'Oh no, no...' the man replied. 'I'm deadly serious.'

'Tell me exactly who you are then.'

'I represent the SOE and, as I explained to Renny, we have a need. And there's no one better suited to the task than the ARCTIC6.'

'Flattery won't get you anywhere,' snapped Iago.

'I'm not trying to flatter,' answered the man, standing up and walking towards the camera, his outline silhouetted against the bright background. 'I couldn't be more serious. We have a situation and we believe you can help us. Now - can we arrange a meeting?'

Iago turned to Cam, who just shrugged. Then he asked Charlie, 'What do you think?'

'Can't do any harm to meet,' she answered quietly.

Tara and Aretha nodded in agreement, which left only me. And Iago knew that there was no way I was going to walk away from a meeting like this. What teenager would?

'We'll go along with this charade for now,' answered Iago, 'but we're not idiots.'

'You are very far from that,' the man replied. 'Now to logistics; I'll send you a secure message in the next few hours with time and place. You don't need to bring anything, just your ears.'

Then he was gone again, and my screen came back to life. As it did, I noticed a small flicker in the top left corner - was someone watching me? *Stop being paranoid, Renny.* It was probably just a tiny glitch caused by the worm.

Shrugging, I turned to face the others. Charlie was first to speak.

'OK, now we've all seen him - is he real?' she asked, studying Iago's face. 'What do you think?'

'I'm not sure, Charl',' he answered. Then he smiled at

her. 'But I'm starting to agree with Cam; this is probably just one of Renny's geeks having a laugh!'

'But what if it really is someone who needs our help?' Tara asked. 'I mean - we can't really turn them down, can we?'

'Let's just go along with it for now,' said Iago.'

'Yeah - can't hurt, can it?' laughed Cam.

The meeting, or rather how we got to it, was actually really cool.

First, I got a message drop through a Playstation forum I administer. That led to another message drop that led me to a well known game site. The message included a couple of cheats to get me through the gameplay. But even with the cheats it took longer than I'd thought to get through. Then the defeated character in the gameplay gave me a coded message that led me through three more online games before I finally got access to the information I needed - the location of the meeting. The whole thing took about six hours, and by the time I'd got the information, we had only thirty minutes to get to the destination.

Iago wasn't very impressed by my slow progress, but then he hadn't been there, had he? I admit that I might have got a bit distracted, but some of those levels were tricky.

We had to head for our local library where we would find further instructions. How cool! This was real spy stuff.

By the time I got the location, Tara and Aretha were already in town and said they'd meet us there. I called Cam - he was at the surf shop, which wasn't far - and

Iago and Charlie set off on foot. I'm not much of a walker. I prefer the bus.

I jumped off the bus outside the library and headed inside. I could see Charlie, idly flicking through something in the literary fiction section. Iago, never far away, was reading something about recording music. Neither of them even glanced in my direction. Hadn't they seen me?

'Psst!' I whispered, walking past Charlie.

She frowned.

Guess they'd noticed me!

'Why are you dressed head to toe in black?' whispered Iago, who'd sneaked up on me from behind.

'What? I often dress like this.'

Well, it's true. Just because they don't usually notice.

'Where are the others?' I asked.

'Don't look now,' said Charlie, 'but Aretha's over in the teen section, and I think I just saw Tara checking out a book on sociology.'

'She's really been getting into that stuff lately,' I said.

'No sign of Cam yet though,' whispered Iago.

'Should I go look upstairs?' I asked.

They both shrugged. I took this as a yes.

The beige carpeted stairs opened out onto a large landing area. All the walls up here were glass, so I could see clearly into each room. To my left was a meeting room with a large, oval-shaped boardroom table, surrounded by comfortable looking, brightly coloured chairs. To the right was a small café area, with that familiar aroma of coffee and chips that all good cafés have. I was suddenly hungry, but a good agent learns to ignore his stomach.

Straight in front of me was the multimedia and archive

section of the library. I could see two of those microfiche machines they use to read archived documents. Surely no one used those things any more? There was a bank of five or six computer screens running along the back wall, and the rest of the room was filled with shelves of DVD boxes and games covers.

I guessed that if anyone were going to meet someone, this would be the best place. It was busy, with lots of teenagers who weren't really interested in anything going on around them; they were just happily discussing this or that game or movie. The librarian was almost invisible behind a stack of boxes and there was a lot of background noise coming from the equipment - this definitely wasn't the quiet room in the library.

I approached the doors slowly, scanning the room. Like I said, no one really stood out in this place. A man, probably around fortyish, was reading the back of a DVD case. He didn't look up when I entered - probably just browsing for a film to rent. I walked on. Rounding a high shelf, I could see a group of kids at one of the games rental shelves. There were five of them, all about my age. One of them glanced up at me. They didn't seem much like government agents. I carried on past them to the next row of shelves. There was no one behind it.

I took a deep breath. Maybe this was all a stupid set-up. Shrugging my shoulders, I turned to leave. Then I noticed a girl at one of the terminals. She hadn't been there when I'd walked in. I could only see her profile, but she looked no more than eighteen. Her black hair was pulled up in a ponytail and, from this angle anyway, she looked really pretty.

I just sort of stood there for a while, staring... not

exactly undercover agent response. Finally, I gathered enough of my wits about me to stumble towards the door. As I passed her, she turned and smiled sweetly at me. She was pretty from this angle too.

'H... hi,' I mumbled.

Great. Now I was a bumbling idiot too! I'd taken a step past her when I heard her say very quietly, 'Hi Renny.'

I froze, mid-step.

'Just sit at the terminal next to mine,' she whispered.

Like an idiot in a trance, I did.

'Just try to look natural,' she said, softly.

My mind went blank - as if suddenly I didn't know what to do with a keyboard.

She frowned.

'He's not responding well,' she whispered into her sleeve. 'What do you want me to do?'

3

I don't know what her boss's response was, but she draped her arm casually over the back of my chair and twirled a loose strand of hair with her finger. I could smell the fresh mintyness of her breath as she leaned in, smiling.

'Renny - don't be frightened. My name is Sarah. Now, look into my eyes. Try to focus.'

I did as she asked, but that just made matters worse. A line from a song I'd often heard my mother singing just popped into my head; something about the sweetest eyes I've ever seen...

'Renny!' Her voice was a bit sharper now.

'Y... yes,' I muttered.

'Where are the others?'

'Downstairs.'

'OK. Stand up. You need to come with me.'

She stood up and, gripping my arm, pulled me to my feet. Then she laughed softly, throwing her head back and put her arm around my shoulders, steering me towards the automatic glass door.

She chattered away about some film she'd seen as we headed down the stairs. It felt like I was watching a film, one of those ones where you're seeing the scene through the eyes of the cameraman. Things were just moving past me, and I couldn't really focus.

Just as we got to the bottom of the stairs, Charlie stepped out into the library's foyer area. The surprised expression in her eyes changed as she sized up my companion.

'Renny?' she said, frowning.

'Charlie,' said Sarah, smiling.

Without breaking her stride, she reached out and linked Charlie's arm in hers.

'So good to see you,' she continued. 'Really, really great. Where's Iago?'

Charlie just nodded in the direction of the main library area.

Sarah smiled again. 'I can't wait to see him, and the girls.'

Iago, who'd obviously been watching, began walking slowly towards us. Turning around, I could see that Tara had spotted us too. She motioned that she was going to get Aretha.

'Now - where's Cam?' Sarah asked brightly, but her eyes betrayed her this time.

Iago frowned. 'I don't know.'

'I'll call him,' I offered, whizzing through the contacts on my phone before anyone else could.

My brother picked up only after the fifth ring. 'Yes?'

'You're supposed to be here, Cam,' I said. 'We're meeting... someone.'

'Is it one of your friends?' he teased.

'No,' I replied. 'It's um... it's a girl.'

'No way!' he laughed. One of your geekfriends knows

a girl? This I have to see. I'll be there in two minutes.'

As soon as I told Sarah Cam's news she headed off to make a private call.

'What do you think?' I asked Iago.

'She's very believable,' he answered. 'But she's probably an actress for hire, Renny. I can just see your geekfriends interviewing every pretty actress in London.'

R ight on time, Cam strolled through the doors, smiling broadly at the rest of us. I rushed up to him.

'What took you so long?' I asked. 'I mean - she's waiting. Sarah's waiting...'

'Relax, Renny,' said my older brother, throwing his arm across my shoulders. 'Now, show me this girl.'

I didn't need to. Sarah had already spotted him and was heading towards us.

'Hi Cam,' she said as she offered her hand. 'I'm Sarah.'

'Cam,' he answered, shaking her hand confidently.

She smiled sweetly at him, then turned towards us.

'Now that you're all together, I can give you the message. You need to find the place where evolution is buried. Your final message is there.'

Then she stepped back and, smiling brightly, said, 'Oh... and you need to stick together.'

With a swish of her ponytail, she turned and walked out of the library.

'Good riddance,' said Charlie.

'What's your problem with her, Charlie?' Cam asked.

'I just don't trust her, with her bouncing ponytail and her perky nose and her fluttering eyelashes,' she muttered.

I'd never heard her talk like that before. Yes, Sarah was bouncy and pretty and sweet, but that wasn't a reason not to trust her.

Was it?

4

'So?' asked Aretha. 'Any of you have any idea what she meant?'

She frowned and Bandit growled quietly, backing her up.

'She said "where evolution died" or something,' said Cam distractedly, his hands busily searching the net on his phone.

'Oh, everyone knows the answer to that!' I said.

They all looked at me.

I stared from one to the other. Didn't everyone know this? I mean, it was just a silly riddle.

'What?'

'Tell us, Renny!' said Iago.

'Well - I presume that evolution refers to Darwin... and she didn't say *died* - she said where evolution is *buried.*'

'So - the place where Darwin is buried?' asked Cam, tapping something into his phone.

I nodded.

'That's Westminster Abbey,' said Cam.

Iago checked the time.

'We could probably be there before four,' he said.

'Train shouldn't take longer than a half an hour.'

'Do you think we need to go there right now?' asked Tara.

My sister looked worried and I knew it was because of her ordeal last year, when Peter Gek had taken her prisoner.

'You don't have to come if you don't want to,' replied Iago.

'But she said that we all needed to be together... remember?' said Charlie.

'Oh yeah,' said Iago. 'You'll have to come along, Tara. But this is probably just some stupid joke. Don't worry - you'll be fine.'

'Yeah, just one of Renny's nerdy geeks trying to impress him,' she replied.

'OK then,' said Iago, clapping his hands together. 'Let's go!'

The train journey to London Victoria passed by in a blur as I went over the events again and again in my mind. I sent out a few messages to some of my geekfriends, trying to find out if they knew anything.

I couldn't tell them about the mysterious man in case he was for real. So all I could do was ask if anyone had any news generally.

As usual, they all got back within minutes. My geeks carried their world with them wherever they went. There were a few who needed big powerful computers, but most of them could do what they needed with a smartphone.

It got me nowhere though. Nobody had ever heard anything strange and they'd hardly admit to it if this were just a prank.

We took the underground from Victoria Station and were at Westminster in minutes. Big Ben towered over us as we came out of the tube exit. I glimpsed the Houses of Parliament as we headed away around Parliament Square. Then the abbey came into view in the distance.

Entering through the West Door, we made our way quietly along the nave. There was no time to admire the stunning beauty of the ancient church. Instead, we headed straight for the left side. I'd been here with my school only last year so I knew where Darwin's grave was. Looking around I could see the others following me, not all as a group - they were being careful not to attract too much attention. Charlie, Aretha, and Tara were slightly behind Cam and Iago. Aretha had had to leave Bandit outside.

As I neared the simple gravestone, I looked around for any clues that might have been hidden in the riddle. Even though I'd racked my brain on the way here, I hadn't been able to discover any. And now I was here, I still couldn't. Would there be a note, a message of some description? A person with instructions? I slowed down a little, allowing my older brother and cousin to catch up.

'What do you think we're looking for?' Cam asked.

He couldn't hide the smirk at the corners of his mouth. He still didn't believe me.

'Could be anything. I think we just have to wait and see,' I answered.

'I'm going to hang back here a bit,' said Iago, indicating a huge pillar to our right. 'Let me know if you see anything.'

He almost kept the grin from his face - he wasn't exactly with me either. My heart began to thump a just little louder in my chest as I walked forward. I didn't want to get my hopes up, in case I was being taken for a ride, but I couldn't help feeling excited. What better place to find mystery and possible adventure?

'Renny,' whispered Cam.

I stopped and whirled around.

He was pointing to something on the floor; just beyond Darwin's gravestone, something shone in the daylight filtering in through the abbey's huge windows. Whatever it was, it was very small. And it was unbelievable that Cam had managed to spot it. If he hadn't taken that exact path, he might never have seen it.

I looked at my brother and raised my eyebrows. He shrugged. Nervously, I made my way across the floor, trying to look interested in Darwin's stone - which I was - but all the time heading for the thing on the floor.

Just as I got within three steps of the stone, a tourist's back materialised out of nowhere. Thick arms stuck out at right angles from his brown and black striped polo shirt. He was taking a photo of someone. As I rounded his huge body, I saw to my horror that the woman he was photographing was standing really close to the spot I was heading for.

I froze. What if she stood on the thing and broke it? What if it became attached to her shoe? I had visions of myself running around Westminster trying to think of a way of separating a tourist from her shoe.

I fought back an overwhelming urge to race towards the woman and guide her away from the area. My legs jittered with impatience as her companion took another photograph.

'Turn a little to your left,' I heard the man saying.

I watched in horror as the woman shuffled slightly, each movement bringing her closer to the object on the floor.

I held my breath.

5

Finally, the man said, 'OK - I think I got everything now. Let's go find some tea.'

'Renny!'

Cam's voice brought me back to the present. Slowly, I stepped towards where he was pointing. As I got close enough I could see the small raised shape on the ground. From this angle, the object didn't reflect the sunlight. It was just a dull, smooth, dark object on the floor. It could have easily been any old bit of plastic, dropped by a tourist.

What if that's all it was?

Pretending to study the gravestone closer, I squatted down, but I didn't reach out to pick the object up straight away. I glanced around first, checking to see whether anyone was watching.

The tourists were still busy being tourists and nobody seemed to be paying me any attention. Now was my time to act.

Like a lizards tongue, my arm shot out and I grabbed the small object. I turned it over in my palm and let out a huge sigh of relief. This was not some piece of tourist trash. This small object was precision engineered. It looked like it came from the research lab of a very high-tech company.

Careful not to damage it, I slipped it into my pocket and stood up. Cam, who'd been watching my every move, motioned for me to come nearer. I walked towards him, trying to look like I had nothing to hide. But my legs were shaking slightly with excitement and an annoying grin kept trying to break out on my face. I had been right. This was not some wild goose chase. Now the others would have to believe me.

Don't lose it now Renny, I told myself. *Just keep it cool!*

An old song popped into my head and I sort of strolled the last few feet in time to it.

'What's with the stupid walk, Renny?' said Cam when I got to where he was standing.

I could feel my cheeks flush. Why was it that when I think I'm being cool, everyone else sees an idiot?

I reached into my pocket for the small object. For one awful second, I couldn't find it. My stomach flipped as my fingers fumbled around and I could feel my heartbeat quickening as Cam's eyes narrowed.

His mouth opened to speak, just as I pulled the small black thing out of my pocket. It was covered in fluff and had a few specks of crisps attached to it. Cam just shook his head before grabbing the object from me.

'Hey!' I cried.

'What d'you think it is?' he asked, ignoring my cry.

'Some kind of device,' I shrugged.

'What do you think it does?' he continued, handing it back to me.

I turned it over in my palm. 'Dunno.'

I'd never seen anything like it before, and believe me; I'm pretty up to date on this kind of thing. I held my palm up, holding the device just in front of my eyes.

As I did, it came to life.

'Cool!' said Cam, as we watched a small 3D laser image grow from a pinpoint in the centre of the flat black device.

'Must be bio-electrically activated,' I said.

Cam frowned.

'It's using the small electric currents produced by my body to run itself,' I explained.

'Can they do that now?' asked Cam.

'Well - it certainly looks like it.'

The 3D image grew until it had become what looked like a large circular pad.

A small scroll undid itself as if being opened by invisible fingers. The tiny message written on it began to magnify itself, until I could read it without squinting.

'What's it say?' asked Cam.

'It's another riddle,' I whispered. '"Time forgets us all, but not he who has no name".'

'Who has no name?' asked Cam, thinking aloud.

'It must be something in here,' I said.

My brother looked around.

'There's not much here except tombstones,' he said.

'Yes,' I answered, thinking hard. 'They're a way of not forgetting, aren't they?'

'I've got it!' said Cam, jumping up.

I'd never seen my brother so excited.

'You can't forget someone if you never knew their name,' he said. 'D'you get it now?'

'Aaah!' I said, grinning at him. 'The Unknown

Warrior. Of course!'

'Sad, huh...' said Cam. 'One of the most visited graves in the world, and no one knows who he is.'

'Let's go and find it,' I said.

Cam checked the map of the abbey he'd picked up on the way in.

'This way,' he said and headed off.

I cradled the device in my hand, following him. Checking over my shoulder, I could see Iago about ten metres behind me. Charlie, Tara and Aretha who had had stopped to look at a painting just to his left joined him.

Cam and I stopped by the tomb of the Unknown Warrior and waited for the others. I thought about the soldier whose remains were buried here and the others he represented and I felt sad for their lost lives.

'Why are we here?' asked Iago, joining us.

'We got a message on this,' I answered, holding the small black device out so he could see it.

He moved his hand over it. As he did, another 3D hologram appeared. This one was different from the first. It formed a dome-shaped pad with six small recesses in which letters began to materialise.

I gasped as I watched the letters appear, one by one, each one set into a small oval recess.

'It's our initials,' whispered Cam.

'Yes,' I replied. 'And those recesses look about thumb-sized.'

'Yeah, they do,' said Cam, nodding his head a few times.

I looked up at him. He looked impressed.

'What are you thinking?' I asked.

'It's just - well, this was designed especially for us. For the ARCTIC 6.'

'Hmmm - that *is* kind of cool,' I said.

'We'd better get the others,' Cam said.

'We're here,' said Charlie, coming up behind us.

'Now I understand why we all had to be together,' I said, showing the device to the others.

I couldn't help but be amazed and more than a bit impressed by anyone who had access to this kind of tech. I mean - this was seriously futuristic stuff.

'What exactly is it?' asked Iago.

'I'm not sure, but it looks like some kind of HapHol... I mean - haptic holographic device,' I replied.

'Some kind of *what*?' he frowned.

'Look, it's not my fault that I know about this stuff and you don't,' I blurted out. 'I won't bother you with it if you're not interested.'

'Sorry, Renny,' said my cousin, smiling. 'It's just that sometimes you seem to know *everything*.'

I'd never heard him admit such a thing before. I felt like a bit of a know-it-all.

'Oh - believe me,' I said. 'There's so much I don't know.'

'Ahem,' interrupted Charlie. 'Renny, please explain to the others what HapHol technology is all about... and quietly.'

She looked to my left, where a group of tourists was milling about.

'OK, OK!' I answered. 'A haptic holograph is a holographic image that allows you to interact with it.'

'But how?' asked Cam.

'Well, they use sound waves - ultrasound - to produce

acoustic radiation.'

I looked around at the others as Tara and Aretha stepped closer.

'Oh no,' giggled Tara. 'Is Renny doing a geek-turn again?'

'Well, to be fair,' smiled Cam, 'we *did* ask him to.'

'Oh, in that case - carry on,' she said, bowing low.

'Well, the acoustic radiation gives the sensation of touch. So, if you see something and reach out to touch it, you get a response. If you push a button, it feels like a button. The data is then fed back through the device, letting it know that you have *pushed* the button.'

'Wow,' said Aretha. 'Sounds really clever!'

'It is,' I replied. 'But what's really amazing about this device is that it shouldn't exist!'

'Why not?' asked Iago.

'Because this technology is in its infancy. They're only supposed to be getting started. I can't believe they could come up with something like this.'

'Do you think we should try it?' asked Tara. 'I mean - it could be dangerous.'

I looked into my sister's dark eyes. She looked a little bit frightened.

'Listen, Tara, I don't think they mean us any harm. And anyway, it's hard to imagine that they could fit anything dangerous into a device this small.'

'Besides,' said Iago, 'this is probably still nothing more than some giant geek-con. One of Renny's friends has probably got a camera trained on us right now. He's probably chuckling into his popcorn as we speak.'

I smiled at my sister.

'Yeah - he's probably right, Tara,' I said. 'Nothing

more than a big prank.'

    I held out the device.

    'So... anyone interested in seeing what happens next?'

6

The crowds inside Westminster Abbey had thinned out somewhat. I checked my watch. Just as I did, the famous chimes of Big Ben piped up. I smiled, listening to the familiar 'Bong'. It was 4 p.m. - teatime for tourists.

I checked all around us - there was nobody near.

'OK - let's do this,' whispered Iago.

I looked at Tara. She smiled. Even though she was nervous, this was getting exciting.

One by one, we began placing our fingers over the appropriate letter on the device in my hand, starting with Aretha, who by now was grinning from ear to ear.

'Just thrilled to be first,' she whispered.

I stepped up next, and a shiver of excitement rushed down my spine. Cam's face didn't change as he casually covered his initial. Tara winked at me as she covered hers. I was glad to see that she was starting to enjoy things now. Iago followed her quickly, then smiled at Charlie.

'What?' whispered Charlie loudly.

I realised that we were all staring at her. Poor Charlie - it was if this whole thing now rested on her shoulders.

'Charlie,' said Iago, 'don't worry. Like I said, this is

probably all one big joke.'

'I know. It's just...'

She took a deep breath, then quickly covered the final letter with her right index finger.

I could hear my own heart thump loudly in my chest and blood pulsed behind my eardrums as we waited for something to happen.

Tara's eyes flitted nervously from face to face. I chanced a glance at Iago, but couldn't read any change of expression on his face. I didn't need to look at Cam - he'd be stony-faced. He's always been good at covering up his emotions.

A faint scraping sound some distance off made my ears prick up, like a dog on alert. The sound seemed to be coming from the back of the nave - the large vaulted hallway behind me.

Iago was already looking directly over my shoulder. Turning my head slowly, I searched for the source of the sound. It was quite dark in this ancient abbey, but I could see that a dark square had appeared in the floor right by one of the ancient walls.

'What is it?' I whispered.

Iago squinted. 'Looks like an opening in the floor.'

'Shall we go and take a look?' I asked.

'Do we all have to stay like this?' asked Tara. 'It might make moving a bit awkward.'

'No,' I said. 'We can't all stay connected. It would be impossible to do anything.'

'Aretha,' said Iago, 'take your finger off the device.'

She did so slowly, carefully. We all glanced nervously at the opening in the floor. Nothing changed.

'Phew,' said Aretha, mopping her brow.

My pulse rate dropped a few notches too. I removed my finger next. Everyone else removed theirs in turn. Once Charlie's finger left the device, the holographic image shrank back into its tiny projector.

'I'll check it out,' said Iago, walking past me.

There was no way I was staying put. As I followed my cousin, I looked behind to see that everyone else was following me. We were all too curious now. We *had* to know what was over there.

The stone right next to the wall had moved back about three feet, revealing an opening in the floor of the abbey's nave.

We leaned in above the opening. Even in the dim light of the abbey, I could see a step. It looked like there was a staircase leading down.

'We're going in there?' asked Tara.

'I think we're meant to,' said Cam, putting his arm around her shoulders.

'Wait,' said Aretha, turning on her heel, 'I'm going back for Bandit.'

'But he's not meant to be in here,' whispered Charlie, looking around nervously.

'Well - I can't leave him outside, can I?' answered Aretha. 'And besides, who wouldn't feel better knowing he's by our side?'

Iago nodded. 'Go and get him then. But make sure no one sees you!'

Aretha crept away quietly, moving through the tourists, stopping a couple of times to look at something. She was good; she was making sure she didn't draw too much attention. Then I remembered the receptionist at the entrance.

'Tara,' I whispered. 'Go and help her. Create a distraction.'

'Oh,' she moaned, 'why do I always have to be the one creating a distraction?'

'Because you're so good at it?'

Her lip curled. I probably should have said that silently.

As we watched Tara go, Cam asked, 'Where do you think that leads?'

'Dunno,' answered Iago, frowning.

'I think this just got exciting,' said Charlie. When she saw the expression on Iago's face, she added, 'Um - in a possibly dangerous and serious kind of way. Or it could still be a joke...'

'This is starting to look a bit less like a geek prank now,' admitted Cam, staring down into the opening.

'Cam - you and Renny go down first,' said Iago.

'Now?' I asked.

'Well, it's better if we go in twos. Less likely to be spotted. Besides, Charlie and I can block you from sight.'

'OK,' replied Cam, then turned to me. 'You got a torch on you?'

'Course I have,' I replied.

Then a thought came to me and, raising my hand, I looked at the small device sitting on my palm. Something told me it didn't just open doors.

'Although,' I grinned, handing the torch to my brother, 'I have a feeling I might not be needing it.'

Cam smiled.

I put the device carefully back in my pocket for safekeeping.

'You first,' said Cam, pushing me gently towards the

hole in the floor.

Suddenly, I didn't feel so brave. Did I really want to be the first to go down there? But I couldn't back out now.

Drawing a deep breath, I placed my right foot onto the first step of the staircase. The steps were really shallow, only about half my foot fitted on the step. Of course, I understood that they had to be shallow. The hole in the abbey's floor wasn't very big. As I put my other foot down, I realised that the steps were also very deep. I had to really bend my right knee before my left foot found the second step. When I looked up, I found that in just two steps, I was almost hip-height with the floor.

Iago and Charlie were standing side by side, with their backs to me, apparently admiring the ceiling.

'It's very steep and the steps are shallow,' I whispered to their backs.

Iago just nodded. I took another step down, now able to anticipate the next step. I found it easily enough and, three steps later, my head was level with the floor.

Before I disappeared undergroud, I caught a glimpse of Aretha in the distance. I couldn't see Bandit anywhere, but Aretha was walking strangely and carrying what looked like her backpack out in front of her. There was no sign of Tara, although I was sure she was close behind.

A cloud of dust made me sneeze. It came from just above my head. Cam must have been right behind me. I reached into my pocket and gently removed the small HapHol device. After a few seconds, it sprang to life again. This time, tiny tendrils of light shone out from it in all directions. The light was really bright, and, unlike a torch, it lit up everything all around me.

Cam stepped down quickly behind me as I moved forward into the low corridor. I just about fitted, but he had to bend his head slightly. He frowned.

'I hate tunnels,' he whispered.

I shivered, hoping there weren't too many rats in this one. I didn't have a problem knowing that they were there, I just didn't want to meet one face to face.

'Move on,' whispered Cam.

Looking behind, I could see more feet coming down the steps. They were Tara's, followed closely by Aretha's. She was still stepping awkwardly, as if she'd lost her balance. Then, as she came into view, I saw why. She was carrying Bandit, who was wrapped in her sweatshirt. He looked so funny. All I could see was his slightly annoyed face sticking out. He clearly didn't appreciate being swaddled like some overgrown baby.

As soon as Aretha made it down the steps, she set the dog down.

'Pheeww!' she said, wiping her forehead on her sleeve. 'It's not easy to carry a dog that's half your own weight, especially if he's struggling the whole time. Bad Bandit!'

The dog moaned softly. He was sorry. He knew he'd annoyed Aretha and licked her hand to make it up to her.

Charlie joined us next, and I could see Iago's feet coming down the steps. That was it - we'd all made it.

As Iago's head cleared the floor line, the HapHol device in my hand changed again. It returned to its former incarnation, with the initials and the finger pads glowing dimly in the dark tunnel.

I realised why at once - the hole in the abbey's floor

needed to be sealed again. Whoever was organising this didn't want random nosy tourists entering the tunnel and discovering their lair.

'Guys,' I whispered.

I didn't need to say any more. The others gathered round me. There was a bit of shuffling and squeezing, but eventually we were all in place. One by one, we placed our fingers in their allotted slots. And again, as Charlie touched the device, the stone above our head moved slowly back into its original position. As it did so, the holographic image disappeared. Through the same small projector, the very bright light reappeared.

There was no turning back now. Although I couldn't be sure, I had a feeling that stone wouldn't open again, even if we wanted it to.

'Ready?' asked Iago, stepping out in front.

'Here, take this,' I said, holding the device out towards him.

The light disappeared as soon as Iago took the device from my hand.

'Weird,' he said, 'it only seems to work when you hold it.'

'Huh?' I said.

Why did I suddenly feel like Shaggy?

'If you don't want to go in front on your own, you could take Bandit,' said Aretha.

Oh great, now I had a Scooby too!

7

After a Shaggy-style gulp, I stepped forward, Bandit by my right knee. I felt a bit foolish, there really was too much light to be scared. But that didn't take away from the fact that we were in a low-ceilinged tunnel underneath an ancient abbey. The tunnel walls looked old too. I started to wonder why the tunnel had been built, and who might have passed through here before me, and what might have happened to them.

'Stop it!' I told myself.

Sometimes it isn't good to let your mind wander. It's a bit like googling stuff. Too much information in the wrong hands can be dangerous.

There was a crunching sound every time I took another step. I looked down. The noise was made by my shoes crushing hundreds of years of grit and tiny pebbles. I tried not to think of where the pebbles might have come from, but I couldn't help imagining thousands of tonnes of earth pushing down on the tunnel's roof. Better to just keep going.

'Where do you think this leads?' asked Tara, from somewhere behind me.

'Probably to some nerd's basement,' said Cam.

'Be serious!' she said. 'How many of Renny's friends could get access to a tunnel under Westminster Abbey?'

'True!' added Aretha. 'They couldn't - could they, Renny?'

'It's very unlikely,' I agreed.

I looked back. Iago was right behind me, his face serious, and I could see Charlie behind him, her head down.

The further we travelled through this dark tunnel, the more obvious it became that none of my geeksquad would have been able to organise this. As we walked on, I got the sense that we were going downhill slightly. The back of my neck tingled. I rotated my shoulders to shrug off the fear that was creeping over me. We were going deeper underground.

As I tried to work out where this tunnel might lead, something to the right of me caught my eye. Bandit, who was on my left, barked loudly. This had the effect of sending me leaping towards the shape instead of away from it. My feet landed no more than six inches from the dark shape, which I could now see was a rat. The rat, in its panic, squealed and ran over my foot, trying to get to the other side of the tunnel. Upon being met by a snarling dog; it turned tail and headed back towards me. I leapt over it, banging my head on the roof of the tunnel.

'Owwww!' I shouted, dropping to my knees.

'Renny, what's going on?' shouted Cam from the back of the group.

By the time I was back on my feet, the rat had disappeared. I glared at Bandit, who just looked at me blankly. There was soft chuckling from behind me.

We trudged on for a few more minutes before Tara called from the back.

'Can you see anything yet, Rens?'

'Um... no!' I replied. 'Just more tunnel.'

'How far do you think we've come?' asked Charlie.

'About a hundred metres,' said Iago.

'How do you know?' asked Aretha.

'I've been counting our paces,' he answered. 'And we've been heading downhill pretty much most of the way.'

'Where do you think we're heading?' asked Charlie.

'I don't know, Charl',' he smiled, squeezing her hand.

'Let's just keep moving,' said Cam. I looked back; Aretha was now in front of him and he had an arm around Tara's shoulder.

After about another fifty metres we came to a junction. We had reached a larger tunnel, which led off into the darkness in both directions. All six of us and the dog stepped out into this more spacious tunnel. We were able to stand in a group and Cam and Iago could stand up straight now.

'Which way?' asked Cam.

'There are no markings on the walls,' said Iago.

'What about the device?' asked Tara.

I looked down. The device remained nothing more than a glorified torch.

'Nothing,' I said.

'Well,' said Charlie, 'I suppose we'll just have to take a chance. If we get it wrong we can always turn back.'

'I'm not so sure,' said Iago. 'Do we know we can open the stone again? Let's just keep going forwards, shall we? Left or right?'

'You choose,' replied Charlie. 'Then at least I can't be blamed if it's wrong.'

'Oh, cheers,' smiled Iago.

'Well, you *are* the oldest,' chipped in Aretha. 'You're the responsible one.'

'All right, all right,' said Iago, raising his hand. 'I'll take the blame if we end up back here in five hours time.'

'By the way,' said Cam, 'does anyone have any water?'

'Or anything to eat?' added Iago.

'Well, I've got some mints,' offered Aretha, fishing in her pockets.

Tara searched her backpack.

'I've got water,' she said. 'It's a few days old, but it should be all right. I mean - in an emergency...'

She dropped her gaze. She'd frightened herself again.

'OK, come on,' said Iago. 'Let's get moving.'

He marched confidently to the left and I followed quickly behind him. He hadn't covered more than two metres when the device in my hand started beeping and flashing red.

'I'm guessing that wasn't the right way,' laughed Iago, turning around.

I shrugged, laughing with him. But I was relieved. At least there seemed to be some point to all this. We weren't just wandering around in some ancient spooky tunnels for no good reason and with no obvious way out.

Bandit dropped back to tag along with Aretha and Tara now that we weren't in single file. He seemed to know that I didn't need him out in front any more. I sighed. I sort of missed our Shaggy and Scooby partnership, now it was over.

Iago dropped back slightly to be with Charlie and Cam joined me out in front.

'Where do you think we're going?' I asked my older brother.

'I've been trying to figure that out,' he replied. 'There are so many famous sites near here that it's hard to choose one. I mean - you've got Big Ben, and the Houses of Parliament within two hundred metres of the abbey. Then you've got Whitehall and Downing Street a bit further along.'

'But we seem to have been walking for quite a while,' I said. 'Surely we've passed those buildings by now?'

'I think you're right,' said my brother. 'Wherever we're heading is further than any of those places. And...'

'And what?' I asked.

He leaned in closer to me, lowering his voice to barely above a whisper, 'I think we're heading in the opposite direction.'

I thought about that for a minute. All the buildings he'd mentioned were slightly to the north of the abbey. And he thought we were heading south. But what was south of Westminster Abbey?

Well there was the whole of South London, but there was one thing between us and that. One massive, unmissable *thing*.

The River Thames.

8

I felt the chill suddenly. Funny how I hadn't noticed it before. I'd been perfectly warm. Now I felt the cold, damp presence of millions of litres of water pressing down on the roof of this tunnel.

I felt the colour drain from my face and turned away from the others so that they wouldn't notice. My heart pounded as some out-of-control fear snaked through my belly. I took a long deep breath, trying to calm it, but just ended up coughing.

'You all right, Renny?' asked Charlie, stepping forward to my side.

I felt stupid. I knew that this was just a panic response.

Tara came over too, offering the water she was carrying.

'Here, Renny,' she said, 'take a drink. Try to relax.'

I took a sip. The cool water had a soothing effect. My muscles relaxed a bit and I was able to control my breathing.

'What's happening, Renny?' asked Tara.

'I... I... dunno,' I muttered. 'Something just - came over me.'

'Listen, guys,' said Iago. 'I think we should just get to

where we are going, quickly.'

Charlie put her arm over my shoulder and we all walked on.

'Can you see something down there?' she asked, pointing straight ahead.

I stared, stretching my arm out, so that the light from the device carried further. The red brickwork of the tunnel's walls funnelled in the distance, but I could see a dark shape at the end.

'It looks like - a door,' I said, though at this distance I couldn't be certain.

'Yes,' replied Charlie. 'That's what I think too!' She turned around. 'Iago - come here.'

My cousin joined us.

'What is it?'

'It looks like a door,' I answered.

None of us spoke for the last few hundred metres of the tunnel. We just walked quietly forward, Iago out in front. We stopped about five metres short of the solid metal door.

'Stay here,' whispered Iago.

We all stood watching as he approached the door. I don't know what we were expecting to happen... but nothing did. He turned, waving us all forward.

'I can't see any locks,' he whispered when we reached him.

'Do you think this can help?' I asked, holding the device up.

'It doesn't seem to be doing anything,' he replied.

I nodded. He was right. The HapHol device just sat there in the palm of my hand, being a light.

'Should we knock?' asked Aretha.

Iago smiled. 'Good question, sis'. What do we think?'

He looked from Charlie to Cam, then at me.

'I dunno,' I shrugged.

'I can't think of anything else to do,' said Charlie.

'Can't hurt,' said Cam. 'I mean, they know we're coming...'

'True,' said Iago, stepping forward.

He banged his fist three times on the door.

9

The HapHol device in my hand suddenly changed back to its original hologram, with our initials appearing one by one.

'Iago,' I whispered loudly.

He came back to join us. Without another word, we all took our positions and placed our fingers on the device. With a clunking sound, the huge metal door began to move to the right.

There was nothing but total darkness beyond the opening, but I could feel a rush of air as the door slowly opened. It was only then that I realised how airless these tunnels had been. I breathed in deeply. It may have been recycled air, but it was cool and refreshing.

I don't know what I'd expected, but it would have been nice if someone had been there to meet us. Instead, we stood there outside the door, looking into the total darkness. Cam peered around the doorway. Iago stayed just behind him.

'Can you see anything?' whispered Tara a little too loudly.

'Shhhhh!' they both replied.

Tara clamped her hand over her mouth.

Cam stepped through the entrance. As he did so, a blinding light silhouetted him in the doorway. That - and the deafening sound of an alarm - made the rest of us freeze where we were.

I threw my hands over my ears to take the edge off the noise and saw that Cam and Iago were doing the same. That noise must have really hurt from where they were.

Finally, the noise died away, and Cam waved us in. My heart drummed in my chest as I walked forward, watching Iago step through the doorway.

'Go on,' whispered Charlie from behind.

'Can you see another door or anything?' Charlie asked.

'No,' answered Cam, who was furthest forward, 'just more of this.'

He made a circle with his finger. I guessed he meant more of what was all round us. We were standing inside a large cavern-like space, which was totally empty.

A booming voice startled us.

'Keep walking forward!'

It came from a loudspeaker system; someone must have fitted this cave with 5.1 surround sound. I looked at my brother. He was looking up, trying to locate the source.

The voice returned. 'At the end of this space you'll find another door. Use the device to open it and you'll be met on the other side.'

Cam and Iago shared a glance, then Cam continued walking. As we followed, a tight feeling snaked across my shoulders and then spread to all the muscles in my upper body.

No one spoke as the smooth metallic door set into the opposite wall of the cavern came into view. And when we got close enough, we all took up our positions around the device without as much as a murmur.

The door opened and I could see a brightly lit corridor beyond it. But still the tense feeling in my shoulders remained. I couldn't relax. This was a serious place.

A man dressed in jeans and a black top stepped into the doorway.

'Follow me,' he said, without smiling or even looking at us.

Swivelling on his heel, he turned and walked away. We had no choice but to follow him. Although I was nervous, I was way too curious to give up now.

Tara caught up with me and caught my hand, squeezing it.

'Are you OK?' I asked.

'I didn't like those tunnels,' she answered. 'But at least we could run and hide in them. Now I feel like we're past the point of no return.'

I knew what she meant, but I didn't want to frighten her by letting it show.

'Try to remember,' I began, 'that they invited us here. We could have said no at any point. So don't worry. They're not going to do anything to us. They obviously need us. Right?'

She was quiet for a few moments, then nodded her head. 'I guess if they'd wanted to harm us, they could have done it at any time.'

'Exactly!' I said, squeezing her hand.

As we followed the guard down another corridor, I tried to work out where we were. The walls looked clean, and the lighting was the modern set-into-the-ceiling type, but there was nothing to give an indication of what kind of place we were in. We could have been passing through the long, unmarked corridors of any big company or government department in London.

'Get in,' muttered the guard, stopping in front of a lift.

'Think we should name him Mr Personality?' whispered Tara as she passed me.

I smiled. My sister has a thing about naming people. When we first met the awful Peter Gek in Suffolk last year, she named him Mr Hollywood Whites because of his gleaming teeth.

'More like Mr Personality Bypass,' whispered Charlie, grinning.

We rode the lift in almost total silence. Bandit panted loudly, his tongue hanging out to the side.

The lift juddered to a halt; the highlighted button indicating that we were on the fifteenth floor. Where on earth were we?

As we followed the guard out of the lift and into another corridor, I tried to work this out. There were windows at the end of the corridor, although the light coming through was quite dull.

I could see another building through the window, and as we got closer I saw a cream wall with a long shelf of dark shiny green glass below it. The colours were very striking next to each other. I only knew of one building in London that was made up of these colours. And, given the direction and distance we'd travelled, I knew I was right.

'Is that MI6?' asked Charlie, before I'd got the chance.

'Yep,' I replied.

'But - why are we in a building beside MI6?' asked Tara.

The door beside us swung open.

'Welcome, children,' came a man's voice from inside.

10

Iago bristled. Calling him a child wasn't making this guy popular.

The room was very dark, with an overhead red glow. I could make out the blue glare of computer monitors and the dark outline of their operators here and there. Only one of these operators turned away from his screen to look at us.

'Come on in,' said a man's voice from the back of the room. 'Don't be shy!'

Bandit growled quietly.

'Come here, boy,' I said softly, tapping my leg.

The dog obeyed, coming to my side, licking my hand. We were a double act again. I had a strange feeling that there was something creepy going on.

'Please, don't be frightened,' the voice continued. 'Come forward.'

Cam, Charlie and Iago entered the room. Aretha and Tara followed, but Bandit and I hung back just a second. I had something up my sleeve... literally! It wasn't anything too fancy, but my sWaP Active watch could record video. I mightn't be able to get much on visual but at least I'd have the audio to listen back to. One of my geeksquad would be able to do something with it, clean it up, isolate something useful. I couldn't begin to imagine what, but there's never any harm in recording stuff.

'Ah, Renny! Good of you to join us,' said the man as we finally entered the room. He was sitting behind a large rectangular glass desk.

'Please, sit down,' he continued.

I could make out six chairs arranged in a semi-circle opposite him. There was very little light. When I looked closer, I could see that the windows were blackened, like those in a posh limousine.

Bandit growled again.

'Shush boy,' said Aretha, crouching down beside him. 'What's got into you?'

The dog just snarled in reply, before barking loudly again. Then he lowered his head but continued growling. A couple of the computer operators turned to look at him. When they did, he laid his ears flat and backed away, barking angrily.

'I'll take him out,' said Aretha. 'I'm sorry. He never usually behaves like this...'

She was right - I'd never seen Bandit do anything like this before. Maybe it was the dark, unsettling atmosphere of the place. It was kind of creepy in there with the blacked out windows and the eerie blue glow.

Aretha took Bandit outside. I could hear her whispering as she left him by the door. He whined softly, but stayed where he was.

'Sorry,' said Aretha. 'He's usually such a good dog. Something must have spooked him.'

She looked at me. 'Might just have been the tunnels,'

she said.

'Maybe,' I answered. But he'd been fine up until now.

'Come and sit down,' said the man, his voice a little louder now

I took a look around; the others were still standing in a group in front of the desk. I hurried towards the middle chair, directly in front of him.

I couldn't see the expressions on the others' faces, but I must have surprised them, because I heard some muttering. They didn't realise that I needed to be directly in front of the man so that I could capture the best possible images and the clearest audio on my sWaP.

'My name is Edward Varken,' said our host, his thin face creasing in a smile.

Now that I could see his face more clearly, he didn't seem so mysterious. Still, he had authorised someone to hack into my system. My smile in reply was a little tight at the edges.

As the others shuffled into the chairs on either side of me, I asked, 'So what is this building then?'

'This...' replied Varken, waving his hand around in a circle, 'is the headquarters of the SOE.'

'It's not up to much,' I said.

'I'd have to agree with you - it doesn't look like much,' he said. 'But - looks can be deceiving, as you will find out.'

He moved his hand over the glass desk in front of him. There must have been a built in sensor, because immediately the surface of the desk came to life. At first, there was just the glow of what looked like a monitor, set flat into the desk's surface. Then before my eyes, a projection popped up out of the screen. I'd seen this kind of thing in Star Wars but never before in real life.

I gasped.

'Wh... what's that?' I managed to mumble.

'Oh - I forgot,' he said. 'You probably haven't seen this kind of holographic screen in action yet.'

'Yes,' I replied. 'That's what I meant.'

Of course, I'd seen videos of holographic screens. I just didn't really expect to see one in use - not yet anyway. The technology was still supposed to be in the trial stages. But then - the HapHol device that had led us here was still supposed to be no more than a twinkle in its designer's eye.

As the 3D holographic map revealed itself, the building in the centre became clear.

11

'That's the MI6 building,' said Charlie.

'Are we in that one?' asked Tara, pointing at the building to the left.

'But that looks like some abandoned eighties' tower block,' said Charlie.

'You're right,' replied Varken. 'But what perfect cover...'

I could see what he meant. No one would ever suspect that this empty, dilapidated shell would house a secret government department that was supposed to have been shut down more than sixty years ago.

'This is a live feed, from one of the many satellites trained on London,' he continued. 'We're here on the fifteenth floor, which from the outside appears to be as abandoned as the rest of the building.'

The holographic image zoomed in to show us the windows of the fifteenth floor. It was true. From the outside, this floor looked no different than the others. In fact, you could see right through the windows. There were no blinds or curtains to block the bird's-eye view.

'Why does this floor look abandoned?' I asked, looking around at all the technology in the room.

'Oh come on, Renny,' said Varken. 'Surely you, of all people can answer that. Or at least hazard a guess.'

'The windows. You're using some kind of masking technology?'

'What kind of masking technology?' asked Tara.

'I'm guessing that the windows are coated with something and they're projecting images on to them, just like a giant television screen,' I said.

'That's about right,' he answered. 'And this is not the only floor we operate on. Obviously all the lower floors are uninhabited. In fact, they are sealed off from the rest of the building by steel-reinforced concrete. However, all the floors above the tenth are... well... SOE HQ. Unofficially, you understand!'

He laughed softly. He clearly liked being under the radar.

'Sarah!' he called out suddenly.

Out of the shadows, the slim familiar figure of the girl we'd met earlier emerged. She strolled over towards the desk we were all sitting around, but stopped just short of it.

'Sarah will outline our situation,' Varken explained, sweeping his arm in her direction.

The girl uncurled something, then attached it to a connection above her head. It looked paper-thin. Once completely unfolded, the paper-like material became rigid and locked itself into a rectangular shape. It was a screen of some sort.

Sarah ran her hand across it and the screen came to life. Again, I'd heard of this kind of technology, but as far as I knew - and I knew *a lot* - it was still at the prototype stage.

I was a little disappointed to find that the image on the screen wasn't holographic. In fact, it wasn't even 3D. The quality was still incredible though, given the fact that the screen could be rolled up like a single sheet of paper.

I had so many questions that my legs were beginning to feel twitchy. How did they operate? Who funded them? Where on earth did they get their tech?

While I'd been busy thinking, it seemed that Sarah had finished preparing her things.

'Is that the NIF facility?' asked Charlie, pointing to an enlarged image on the screen.

Hmmmm... maybe I should have paid more attention to what was going on.

'Don't be rid—' I started but luckily for me, Sarah intervened.

'Yes it is,' she said, looking around at the group.

'Why are you showing us that?' I asked.

'More importantly,' said Iago, 'what is the NIF?'

'Do you want to? Or shall I?' asked Sarah, smiling widely at me.

I couldn't think for a moment, never mind answer her. I just sat there. Luckily it was quite dark, so my burning cheeks probably couldn't be seen.

'OK,' said Sarah, taking my silence as a no. 'The National Ignition Facility is located in Livermere, California.' She paused, looking around at our faces. When nobody reacted she continued, 'I'm not a scientist, but I'm told that the aim of the NIF is to create energy from nuclear fusion. Their motto is "Bringing Star Power to Earth".'

'Oh, wait!' said Aretha. 'I know about this. Or, well, I

mean - I've seen a TV programme about this.'

'Then you probably know that the aim of the NIF is to create cheap clean energy,' answered Sarah.

Aretha nodded, smiling.

'The facility was officially completed in 2009,' Sarah continued, 'and they hope to have what they call "net energy gain" very, very soon.'

'What does "net energy gain" actually mean?' asked Tara.

I looked at Sarah. I could probably explain this better than she could.

She nodded.

'It means,' I said, turning to my sister, 'that they hope to produce more energy from the reaction than they had to put in to get it started.'

'That sounds sensible,' said Tara. 'There wouldn't be much point in using up more energy than you can produce.'

'Yeah,' laughed Aretha, 'that'd be like energy reduction.'

'Listen...' interrupted Varken, 'I'm sure that you're all very smart kids and that I don't have to explain to you that the world needs to find an alternative to fossil fuels like coal and oil.'

'We all know that oil reserves are limited,' said Tara.

'Yes,' he replied. 'The fact is that all fossil fuel will eventually be used up, possibly within thirty years. We've known this for a very long time.'

'That's why places like the NIF were set up,' I added. 'And last I heard they'd achieved the first step towards "ignition".'

'That's right, Renny,' said Sarah.

I even liked how she said my name. I felt myself blushing again.

Varken leaned forward in his seat so that I could see his face in the dim light from the screen. He had deep creases in his forehead, and dark circles around his eyes.

He sighed, then said, 'Unfortunately, we have a massive problem!'

12

'What kind of problem?' asked Iago, turning away from the screen.

'Well,' said Varken, 'as Sarah said, we are not scientists here. But we do have some, how shall I put it - very reliable experts.'

I believed him. He probably had access to the greatest minds on the planet.

'Come in, Professor,' said Varken, raising his voice slightly.

A panel door on the side wall slid back, revealing a figure.

The man was tall and thin, and quite unmistakable. He's been on our screens so much in the last few years that I'd have recognised him anywhere. His TV shows really bring science to life, for adults as well as kids. Charlie gasped and Iago mumbled something to Cam.

My jaw dropped. This man has forgotten more about nuclear physics than I will ever know.

'Ryan Green!' I said, rushing towards him, holding out my hand. 'Wow! I mean... *Professor* Ryan Green... It's such an honour to meet you.'

'Hey, Renny,' he replied, in his familiar friendly

style, 'the pleasure's all mine.'

This was just surreal. Not only did he know my name, but he seemed pleased to meet me.

'Hi everyone,' he said, smiling at the others.

Cam mumbled hello. Iago grumbled something. I turned around to see Tara smiling shyly back at him and Aretha hold her hand up in a silent greeting. But Charlie stood up and took a step nearer.

His smile widened as she approached, and the room lit up. It was easy to see what made him so popular - aside from his brilliant brain, that is.

'Hi,' said Charlie, holding out her hand, while at the same time pushing a stray lock of hair behind her ear.

'You must be Charlie,' said Professor Green, looking down at her.

He'd done his homework - he knew about Charlie too.

'Listen,' interrupted Varken, 'we don't have time for polite introductions. Professor Green is a very busy man. Now, let's just assume that you all know who he is, and be assured that I've briefed him on all of you and your particular - skills.'

'Shall I?' asked Professor Green, stepping over to the screen.

Now it was Sarah's turn to blush. She stepped aside, her eyes cast downwards.

'As Mr Varken said, there seems to be a problem with the science at the NIF - in particular at the LIFE machine, and possibly also at ITER, a sister project in France.'

He looked around, waiting for the question.

Aretha obliged him, raising her hand. 'What is the LIFE machine?'

'The LIFE machine is a Laser Inertial Fusion Engine. Basically, it's a prototype of a power plant that will eventually be used to produce energy from nuclear fusion.'

'But don't we already have nuclear energy?' asked Aretha.

'Yes we do,' replied Professor Green. 'But we generate energy by splitting open the nucleus. That's called nuclear *fission*. And although it's relatively easy, there are serious side-effects of splitting atoms.'

'Yeah, like nuclear waste!' spat Tara.

'Exactly,' said Professor Green.

'So - this fusion - it doesn't create nuclear waste?' asked Aretha.

'It should provide clean energy. In fact, the scientists at LIFE even believed they could use spent nuclear fuel in the LIFE machine,' replied Professor Green.

'Why are you talking about all these things in the past tense?' asked Iago.

Green lowered his gaze. For a few moments, he said nothing, just stared at the floor. Then, raising his eyes, he looked from one to the other.

'I almost don't want to say this...'

He paced back and forth, his head down. You could have heard a pin drop. Finally, he raised his head, looking from one of us to the other.

'Certain evidence has come to my attention recently that leads me to believe that there could be a fundamental flaw in the scientists' calculations.'

'What kind of flaw?' asked Cam.

'A big one,' replied Professor Green. 'I mean... earth-shatteringly big.'

'I'm guessing you don't mean that in a positive way,' I said.

'No,' he replied. 'I mean it in the most literal way.'

'What? Like the Earth could actually shatter?' asked Aretha.

'Yes,' he replied. 'At the NIF they talk about creating a 'Star on Earth'. Well, *if* they've got it wrong they could create a *Killer Star*... a star that could supernova and destroy the planet.'

13

I gasped and looked around at the others. Even in the dim light, I could see the shock on their faces.

'Look guys,' Professor Green continued, 'you've come up against this kind of potential before. So you know that there are things out there that really could destroy the planet. And at the NIF, there are such things.'

'Yes,' I answered on behalf of everyone, 'we do understand.'

I'd seen the power of nuclear physics before. We'd had to stop a madwoman from trying to destroy the world using the Large Hadron Collider at CERN.

'What is the flaw in their calculations?' I asked.

'I can't be sure, Renny,' answered the scientist. 'I'd need to check through everything to be absolutely sure, but from what Mr Varken's people have shown me, it looks like a massive error.'

'Thank you, Professor Green,' interrupted Varken. 'I know that you're keen to start working through all the maths, so please don't let us keep you any longer. There's a lab on the seventeenth floor at your disposal. And please don't hesitate to let me know if there's anything you need.'

'But—' I began.

'Renny. I know you're curious, but Professor Green needs to get started on his work.'

Varken clicked his fingers and an SOE agent who'd been by the door came forward.

'This way Professor,' said the man, politely showing Green to the door.

Green began to walk towards the doorway but stopped halfway, turning back. He opened his mouth to say something, but then stopped. Shaking his head slightly, he carried on out of the room. I was left wondering what he was thinking, and wished we could have had some more time together.

I was jerked out of this train of thought by Sarah's voice. She had returned to the screen.

'OK, guys. Let's assume that Professor Green's research proves what we suspect.' She looked around at us before continuing. 'The big problem we have is that, after years of preparation and set-backs, the LIFE machine is set to do its first *live* test next week. And although ITER isn't yet fully operational they don't want to be left behind, so they're planning something similar, but on a smaller scale.'

'So, if there's a flaw in their calculations, why are they going ahead?' asked Iago.

'Because they don't believe the scientist who spotted the flaw,' said Varken.

'Why not?' I asked.

'Well,' continued Varken, 'he's a nobody - only just finished his Masters degree.'

'So why do you believe him?' asked Iago.

'He came highly recommended,' replied Varken

sharply. 'And when our scientists looked through his work, they believed him. That's why we contacted Professor Green. No one will doubt *his* authority on the subject.'

'So why doesn't Professor Green just talk to them?' Charlie asked.

'Professor Green has only just been given the details,' replied Varken. 'He's not about to go accusing fellow scientists of making a mistake. Not until he's checked everything thoroughly. Can you imagine what would happen? Even if our evidence is correct, there'd be an outcry from the eminent scientists at the facility. No one wants the world to know they've made a fundamental error.'

'And, if you're wrong,' I interrupted, 'Professor Green's reputation would be trashed.'

'Exactly,' Varken replied. 'So we need to allow the Professor to take all the time he needs to check the results.'

'I still don't see what this has to do with us,' said Iago.

Varken inhaled deeply, his nostrils making a whistling sound. He leaned forward, placing his elbows on the desk, steepled his hands, and let his chin rest on his fingertips.

'We need a plan B.'

'What do you mean?' asked Cam.

Varken raised his head.

'If the scientists refuse to back down, we may need you to destroy the LIFE machine.'

14

'So we're your Plan B?' I asked.

It was pretty obvious really. I mean - why else would we be there?

'What exactly do you think we can do?' asked Iago.

'I can't really reveal those details yet,' answered Varken. 'But we will need you to place some devices at both facilities which will allow us to shut down the machines if the scientists don't halt the tests.'

'That's not enough information,' snapped Iago, standing up and backing away from the desk.

'No, no, no. You misunderstand me. I can't be more specific at the moment, we don't have the intel we need.'

'What intel?' asked Cam.

'Look - at the moment we've got a team checking out the facility. Some of them are working undercover on site, and on the floor above us we've got our computer operatives checking through everything from building blueprints to staff rotas. We can't formulate our plan until we know more about the place. But what I can say is that we need you ready to go at the drop of a hat.'

'But why us?' asked Tara. 'I mean - surely there's someone more experienced than us.'

'Of course we *do* have adult operatives,' he replied. 'But for this mission we need people who can pose as students.'

'Why not choose some students then?' asked Iago.

'Like I said,' Varken replied, 'ARCTIC6 have a special skill set.'

Iago looked unconvinced.

'Look,' said Varken, standing up suddenly. 'I'm not trying to hide anything from you. I don't have all the details yet, but we need your help, and I'm asking you now, on behalf of the people of this country. In fact, possibly on behalf of the people of the *planet* - will you *help* us?'

He banged his fist on the desk for the last word of this speech. I jumped. Varken slumped down into his chair again, puffing his cheeks out.

'I'm sorry,' he said, waving one hand towards us, using the other one to wipe his brow.

I felt suddenly guilty and looked at Iago, who was looking down at the floor, even though in the dim light of the room the floor couldn't be seen.

'I suggest,' said Varken, raising his head, 'that you all go home now and I'll contact you when we have all the information we need.' He shook his head then added, 'I suppose all I really want to know is - if push comes to shove, can we call on you?'

He sounded weary, almost defeated. I couldn't see his face, but I felt a lump building in my throat.

'OK,' said Iago quietly. 'But the first sign of anything strange - we walk!'

'Thank you,' whispered Varken.

'So how do we get out of here?' Aretha asked.

'Back the way we came?' suggested Tara.

My throat tightened painfully. I was going to have to go under the billions of tonnes of water that was the Thames again. And this time it would be even worse - there'd be all the build up and nervousness beforehand.

Stay calm, Renny, I said to myself. I couldn't let these people see me fall apart. If they did, then I was pretty sure they'd manage to find me a desk job while the others went out and had the adventure. I wasn't getting left behind this time. Everyone knew I was the 'brains' of the outfit, but that didn't mean I was a wuss.

'Yes,' replied Varken, 'you cannot be seen leaving here. In fact, no one can be seen leaving here.'

'But surely they don't all leave through Westminster Abbey?' said Charlie.

'Oh no,' laughed Varken, 'that *would* be a sight, wouldn't it? No - that's a civilian portal. There are a few other ways of accessing this building; some of them very close by.'

He didn't need to point. We all understood.

I wondered how many of the 'staff' entering the MI6 building next door were actually SOE operatives.

'Sarah will guide you back to through the tunnels,' said Varken. 'Once you're out, she'll bring back the device. After I've arranged the next stage, she will be your only point of contact with this agency. Understood?'

He looked around at us all and smiled.

'When will you contact us again?' asked Iago.

'As I said,' replied Varken, 'time is of the essence. The LIFE machine is due to start up next week, if not sooner. If we're not successful in persuading the scientists to halt their tests then we'll need to act quickly. So don't go anywhere. I'll be in touch probably within the next few hours.'

'That soon?' said Charlie. 'What are we going to tell our parents? I mean we can't just sneak out in the night!'

'I've heard you've done that kind of thing before,' said Varken.

'Yeah, but... that was different,' replied Charlie.

'I know,' said Varken. 'If we need you, we'll come up with a cover story. Remember, we're quite good at that.'

'Guys,' said Sarah, 'we need to get going. Otherwise you might end up spending the night in the abbey.'

Nobody else said a word, but we were all by the doorway in the blink of an eye - me bringing up the rear, as usual. I couldn't help glancing back over my shoulder as I waited for the others to make their exit. As I did, the man at the computer terminals who'd checked us out earlier turned towards me. With only the dim blue light coming from his screen, I could barely make out his face, but he smiled - a kind of a tight, closed-mouth smile.

For some reason, the hairs on the back of my neck stood up.

15

All the way down in the lift, I tried to work out why I'd reacted that way to the shadow-man's grin.

'You're quiet,' said Tara, punching me lightly in the arm. 'Come on, Rens, what's going through that *extraordinary* brain of yours?'

My sister's teasing always makes me smile.

'Actually, not a whole lot, sis',' I replied. 'I just had a strange feeling about something - that's all. Probably nothing!'

'This whole thing kind of gives me the creeps,' she said softly.

'Yeah - me too. My imagination's getting the better of me today.'

The lift pinged and I was glad to be moving again. Too much time to think isn't good for someone like me. Sometimes I wish that I didn't understand so much. Like when I imagine a train crashing into another train, I can calculate the force at the point of impact. And then I can't stop myself thinking about what effects it might have on the people on board. I try to stop myself from doing this, but it's not always easy when you know how things work.

We followed Sarah back along the corridor towards the room that led to the tunnel. I studied her back as she led the way. Maybe I should ask her about her boss? Iago must have been thinking along the same lines, because he fell into step beside her.

I caught up with Charlie.

'What do think of it all, Charl?' I asked.

'It's sounds pretty real to me. I mean - that there could be an error, that the star could supernova.'

'I agree,' I said.

'But I just don't trust her,' she said nodding towards Sarah's back. 'Not since the moment I saw her.'

'She seems perfectly nice,' I said.

'Exactly what I mean. She's got all of you under her spell.' Charlie leaned in closer. 'Listen, just because she's pretty and she's sweet doesn't mean you can trust her. All right?'

'OK, Charl,' I said.

I didn't want to argue any more, so I decided to change the subject.

'So what about Varken?' I asked.

'I don't know, Renny,' she said. 'It just all seems kind of surreal. I mean - why would anyone need the help of a group of teenagers?'

'Some of us aren't even teenagers,' I said, looking back at Aretha and Tara.

'Yeah, but only an idiot would underestimate those two,' smiled Charlie, following my gaze.

Aretha grinned at us. She's braver than most teens I know.

With the light from the cavern filtering into the old tunnel, Sarah stepped through the doorway, followed by Iago, then Cam. Charlie and I hung back, allowing Aretha and Tara to go ahead of us.

'I suppose if I needed to send some young people on an undercover mission, I'd probably choose us too,' I said.

'Yeah,' laughed Charlie, 'we *have* been pretty successful at getting things done in the past.'

When we finally emerged, Cam was standing next to Sarah, with Iago waiting on the opposite side of the opening.

'Do we need the device to shut the door?' I asked, joining the others.

'No,' answered Sarah. 'The door will close automatically, but you'll need to use it as a light.'

'Oh... of course,' I said, holding the device in my open palm.

It flicked on straight away. She smiled, and turned away. Cam followed, immediately falling in step with her. I couldn't hear their conversation but his face was lively, and he was waving his hand up and down in a swishing motion. I kind of got the feeling that he was talking about surfing. To be honest he doesn't talk about much else.

'So - did you manage to find out anything useful?' Charlie asked Iago quietly.

'Not much,' muttered Iago. 'She's pretty tight-lipped about her boss. Says he's a good guy...'

'She would say that,' said Charlie.

She was frowning again. Sarah couldn't do or say anything right in Charlie's book.

'Got to go and ask Aretha... um... something,' I said.

I felt as stupid as I sounded but I just wanted to get

away from them - give them some space. I headed towards Tara and Aretha.

Bandit licked my hand as I put my arm around Aretha's shoulders. They seemed to be friends again after his funny turn in Varken's control room. Not that I blamed him; I'd had a weird encounter there too! I patted his head and he nuzzled against my leg. Any friend of Aretha's was a friend of his. You definitely wouldn't want to be her enemy though. He'd do anything for her; I've seen him in action.

'Friction?' asked Aretha, nodding towards Iago and Charlie.

'Yeah - Charlie's really got a thing about Sarah,' I whispered.

'It's kind of hard to miss,' whispered Aretha. 'Although I have to say, I can see why.'

'Yeah, me too,' I said. 'Charlie's used to being the pretty one, getting all the attention. It must be hard to have to share it after all this time.'

'That's not what I mean,' said Aretha. 'It's just that Sarah's got all three of you drooling over her.'

'I did not drool!' I said.

Aretha grinned, raising her eyebrows.

'OK, OK. So there may have been drooling,' I admitted. 'But to be honest, I think Sarah should be the least of our concerns.'

'What do you mean?' asked Aretha.

'Did I say that out loud?' I said. 'Don't pay any attention to me, cuz. I'm just babbling.'

'What should we be worried about, Renny?'

My cousin wasn't giving up.

'Dunno - just some guy at the SOE looked at me,

that's all. Gave me the creeps.'

'But why?'

'There was something familiar about him.'

'What was it?' she asked.

'It was dark, so I can't be sure... but it was definitely something...'

16

Going back under the river wasn't as terrifying as I'd feared. Having Sarah around made me feel more relaxed. Nothing bad would happen to me when she was around.

Cam had joined Iago and Charlie, so I decided to try to get some information out of Sarah about the people she worked for. From what I'd heard none of the others had found out anything useful.

'Hi,' I said, falling into step beside her.

'Hi, Renny,' she replied, smiling.

'So, what's it like working for Varken?' I asked.

'Look, Renny,' she smiled. 'I'm not trying to upset you or anything, but I *am* a trained SOE agent. So your interrogation skills aren't likely to work - are they?'

'Hey! I wasn't asking you to break the Official Secrets Act, or anything,' I said. 'Surely, you understand my... um... concerns? We may be just six "kids", but we've managed to achieve some pretty amazing things so far.'

Sarah looked away. When she looked back, her eyes were softer.

'Look, Renny,' she began, 'I'm not trying to disrespect you in any way. It's just that, well - I can't talk about my boss, or my job, or anything. I just can't!'

That was that, then. There was nothing to talk about.

I was about to drop back - just let her drift ahead, when she spoke again. 'By the way, I think what you do is pretty cool, you know. I've been following the ARCTIC6 for a while now. All that stuff with turning a satellite around and your geeksquad getting into systems when the chips were down, tracking planes and broadcasting stuff. It's pretty amazing really!'

'Oh, thanks!' I could feel my cheeks burning as I spoke.

'That's why we need you,' Sarah continued. 'This operation, it... well, it needs someone to take a different approach. Because of the timeframe, we can't use adult operatives. Normally, for an operation like this an agent would have to be given a cover story and be in place for a few weeks. They'd have to earn the trust of the people running the facility. Because the live test is scheduled for next week, we don't have time. We need someone who can walk in through the front door without raising suspicions. We need people who can pose as students and no one will ever suspect otherwise.'

I understood.

'See - that wasn't so bad,' said Aretha, clapping me on the back.

I wheeled around to face her. 'What wasn't?'

'I mean - you didn't freak out like you did on the way over.' She looked from my face to Sarah's, then backed away mouthing, 'Sorry.'

To Sarah's credit, she didn't push me to tell her what exactly Aretha was talking about, but from the look on her face, she didn't need to. They'd probably had a visual on us the whole time we'd been in the tunnel. I was probably lower than an amoeba in her opinion, no matter what she thought of my geeksquad's abilities.

'So,' I began, 'when do you think Varken will be able to let us know whether he needs us or not?'

'If I had to guess, I'd say this evening or tomorrow,' she replied. 'Gives his guys enough time to gather and digest the intel. And, hopefully, Professor Green will have had time to evaluate the science too.'

'It gives me a bit of time to do some checking too,' I said.

'But it could be sooner, so be prepared,' she added. 'And not a word of this to anyone. Not Dragosh, not Aaron - no one, understood?'

The force in her voice surprised me a little, as well as the fact that she knew the names of my top geekfriends. She could be scary, when she wanted to be.

'I wasn't planning on telling anyone,' I answered.

We plodded on in silence until we came to the turn off for the abbey.

'What's down that way?' I asked, pointing in the direction we'd nearly gone earlier.

'Just access to some other buildings,' she replied, waving her hand.

'OK,' I said.

Clearly, she wasn't going to tell me anything I didn't need to know.

Aretha and Bandit joined me.

'What d'ya think's down there, Rens?' whispered Aretha.

'I don't suppose we'll ever find out,' I replied.

17

When Aretha and I reached the stone steps that led up to the abbey, Sarah was waiting. The others all joined us and quickly we stepped into position. It seemed that nobody wanted to hang around in these dark, ancient tunnels any longer than they had to.

Carefully, I held out the device. It felt kind of grail-like in my hand - powerful despite its fragile appearance. As it came to life, I looked up at the circle of my friends. With their eyes cast down towards the device and its eerie glow on their faces, they could have been involved in some religious ritual. In another time and place they could have been worshipping the small device.

My hands shook but I managed to get my finger into its socket on the device. Again when Charlie placed her finger against the device, the old stone in the abbey's floor began to move.

'It's almost closing time,' whispered Sarah. 'There shouldn't be any visitors about to see you, but the staff won't have left yet, so you should be able to get out. If you're questioned, just say you got lost.'

Then she smiled. She knew that she didn't really need to tell us how to evade capture.

'I'll go check it out,' whispered Charlie, always the brave one.

We all watched her disappear up the steep steps towards the dim rectangle of light above. She stopped near to the top of the stairs, then carefully poked just the top of her head through the opening. Gripping the edges of the rectangle for balance, she pivoted around to check behind her.

Like a sprinter out of the blocks, she pounced up the last few steps and out of sight. A moment later, her head peeked back over the edge of the hole.

'It's OK,' she whispered. 'Come on.'

'You go next, Tara,' said Cam.

Aretha slipped into position just behind her. For some reason I stayed rooted to the spot, just watching as the others made their way up the old stone steps.

When Aretha had almost reached the top, she turned back, a worried look on her face.

'Bandit!' she hissed. 'Where are you?'

I looked around and was surprised to find the dog behind my legs. If I didn't know better, I'd have sworn he was hiding.

'What d'you think you're up to?' I asked.

The dog just cocked his head to one side and let out a small doggy yelp.

'Looks like he's sticking with you,' smiled Sarah.

'He doesn't normally do that.' I frowned.

Who knew what was going on in a dog's mind? Images of dogs prancing through the surf in the sunshine, then racing to lick their owners hands lovingly, flitted through my mind. What was going on in *my* head?

'Come on then, fella,' I said, reaching down to grab

his collar.

I couldn't believe it when he wrenched himself away from my hand, then growled and ran off back down the tunnel.

'No Bandit... no!' cried Aretha.

I looked up towards the opening. 'Don't worry, Aretha - I'll go and get him back. Probably just having a funny turn.'

I smiled at her, but I was a bit worried. Bandit always preferred to be with Aretha. He was her dog. What was the idiot playing at?

I'd walked no more than two paces away from the opening when the scraping sound from above my head made me freeze like a statue. Nervously, I turned my head, only to see that the stone was moving back into place. I looked at Sarah. She frowned, pointing to the device.

'It's programmed to seal the exit as soon as it moves away from it. It should have been me carrying it, though, not you.'

Of course! Sarah was meant to take the device back to the SOE building. The device didn't know that it was me carrying it and not her.

'But we need to stop it!' I said.

'We can't,' she answered. 'It's programmed so that all six of you need to be there to activate it.'

I looked up at the ever-decreasing rectangle of light above us. Even if they all dived headfirst down the opening, they wouldn't make it in time.

'Renny!' Iago whispered loudly.

'Just go,' I answered. 'I'll find a way out. You don't want to get locked in.'

'OK, but let us know as soon as you're out.'

The stone moved back into its final position.

The device glowed softly, lighting up a circle around us. I gazed at it, as it grew brighter. I could feel the corners of my mouth drawing down as I stared up at the huge stone that separated me from the others.

Sarah took my arm gently.

'Don't worry Renny, we'll get you out.' She turned around, looking back the way we'd come. 'But first, we need to find that foolish dog of yours.'

In a kind of dream, I followed her down the tunnel. We didn't speak and there was no sound other than the familiar crunch of hundreds of years of dirt under our feet.

'Bandit, where are you?' Sarah called softly.

There was no reply from the dog. I felt so sorry for Aretha. Why was he doing this?

'Bandit,' I called softly, my voice echoing in the creepy tunnel. 'Bandit?' I called again, jogging past Sarah.

She upped her pace to keep up with me. Although I tried not to show it, by the time we reached the section where the tunnel split, I was starting to run out of breath.

'We'll need to split up,' said Sarah, looking up and down the dark space.

'But there's only one of these,' I panted, holding up the device.

'Some of us do come prepared,' she smiled, fishing a normal torch out of her pocket.

'OK,' I said, 'I'll take this direction.'

I hoped that the sound of my voice cracking was only in my imagination.

'OK,' she replied and immediately sprinted off the opposite way.

I have to admit that I was slightly relieved - there was no way my geek-physique would have lasted another hundred metres. But the relief slipped away pretty quickly as I faced the other tunnel - alone.

18

A sudden breeze lifted the hair behind my right ear. Funny - I hadn't noticed any wind before. In fact, the tunnels had felt airless, stuffy even.

As I started to imagine what could have caused this breeze, the hairs on the back of my neck tingled again. I gulped loudly and froze mid-step. Was there something following me? Did I dare to turn around? Did I want to know what was behind me? Was it better to face the threat or run away as fast as I could?

I decided that, given my fighting ability (none), it was probably better to just run away. Although this didn't improve my chances of survival much, since whoever or whatever was chasing me would catch up with me in the end. I was doomed either way.

I was sure I could hear a dull thud, almost like an echo every time one of my feet hit the ground. Course, this was a tunnel, so echoes were to be expected, but they weren't exactly in time with my footsteps. It sounded like another human trying to copy my pace.

Beads of sweat from my forehead trickled over my eyebrows, seeping down, stinging my eyes. I tried to make out what was up ahead, but all I could see were the gloomy tunnel walls, studded with darker recesses, closing in on each other. As my feet continued to pound down the tunnel, my eyes scanned the horizon for any change in the structure. I thought I saw something at the end. It might be an exit! I quickened my pace, sprinting now, desperate to get out of this place.

My heart drummed louder. My chest began to hurt as my lungs sucked in oxygen. If I didn't find a way out soon, I'd have to stop.

With my head down, I raced forwards. There was definitely an opening in the right-hand tunnel wall. Maybe not an exit, but at least I'd be out of this tunnel. Just a few more steps.

As my right foot rounded the corner of the opening something exploded on to me, knocking me flat on my back. I hadn't even had time to open my eyes.

I'm not afraid to admit that the scream that came from my mouth was one of pure, animal, howling terror.

I lay there panting for a moment, afraid now to open my eyes. Then I heard a sound that was very, very familiar. It was something that I'd heard many times, and none of those times had ever been bad.

'Bandit!' I whispered, opening my eyes.

'Woof,' he replied, then growled again.

I bolted upright. Why was he still growling? I followed his gaze. He was growling at something around the corner in the tunnel I'd just left. Now I knew that the footsteps I'd heard hadn't just been in my imagination. There *was* someone following me. And it seemed like they were still there.

I jumped up. I could see a dark, square shape at the end of this tunnel. It must be an exit!

'Let's go, boy,' I shouted.

Bandit wagged his tail. This time he was coming with me. He didn't like whatever was down there either.

'Not so brave now?' I teased as I started running away from the direction of the footsteps.

He kept his head down and trotted along beside me.

'What was all that about anyway?' I asked. 'Why did you go running off like that?'

He just growled. I had no idea what he meant, but I suppose it was instinct that sent him off down that tunnel. I was glad now that he had. The person following me had probably been lying in wait for Sarah. She was meant to be travelling back through these old tunnels on her own.

At least he was following *me* now - Sarah was safe. Then it hit me. I was running away from that person. What would they do if I escaped? They'd be back to where they started. They could turn their attention back to Sarah!

I stopped dead. Bandit shot past me, stopping a couple of bounds later. He dropped his head to one side, looking into my eyes.

'It's no good, boy,' I said, 'we have to go back.'

He just continued staring into my eyes.

'We can't leave her here - alone.'

The dog surprised me by walking up and licking my hand. I didn't know if this was because he understood me, or just because he thought I needed a lick. Either way, I appreciated it.

I jogged back towards the junction with the main tunnel. I was beginning to hate this place. Even the bats hanging from the roof of the tunnel gave me the creeps -

and I like bats. The steady drip of a leaky pipe sounded cold and hard.

As I got closer to the junction, I heard the faint but unmistakable rhythm of someone running in the main tunnel. They were heading towards the same corner I was, running very softly, but the dull thud of their feet echoed all along the tunnel.

What should I do?

I looked behind me, my heart pounding. The exit seemed very far away now. Should I turn tail and hope I reached it before they rounded the corner? What if I made it all the way there, only to find it wasn't an exit? Or if it was an exit - that it was locked? It was most likely to be locked. I mean, the other exits had been locked, hadn't they? These were tunnels that led to very, very secret places. They'd hardly be left unlocked. Oh no, my brain was babbling. *Breathe, Renny! Get a grip, get a grip, get a grip!*

I could feel waves of panic rising in my stomach. I looked left to right then back to the left again. What should I do?

I felt the hairs on my neck move up, sending a shiver down the centre of my back. Beads of sweat began to spring from just below my hairline.

As the footsteps drew closer, my knees started to feel weak and I had to concentrate quite hard to keep my legs straight. I pressed myself tight against the wall as the owner of the footsteps came close enough that I could hear the crunch of grit beneath their feet.

The volume of my pounding heart suddenly went up, sending blood spurting around my body. The valve closest to my ears banged open as the blood pounded through it. I was beginning to feel light-headed.

I held my breath, as my pursuer took the last few steps towards the corner.

Time slowed down. The sound of the footsteps seemed longer and lower than it had before.

Bandit stood beside me against the wall, ears cocked, teeth bared, ready to pounce. I took a couple of deep breaths, clenching and unclenching my fists. I heard the crunch of grit on the tunnel's floor as the footsteps got ever closer.

With a wolf's howl, I leaped away from the wall and hurled myself around the corner. I collided with my pursuer mid-leap and we both tumbled to the floor, clinging to each other in a wrestler's embrace.

19

'Renny - what on earth are you doing?'

I looked down at Sarah, on top of whom I now lay sprawling, arms and legs flapping like a giant squid.

'Oh, sorry,' I mumbled, shuffling myself to the ground as quickly as I could.

She dusted off her top, then fixed me with a stare.

'I thought you were someone else,' I muttered.

'What do you mean?' she asked. 'There's no one else down here.'

'Well, someone was following me,' I answered.

'Oh, don't be silly,' she said, looking away. 'It's just your imagination playing tricks. It can be a bit spooky down here on your own.'

She jumped up and added cheerily, 'At least you found this naughty dog.'

Bandit growled.

'Hey boy,' I said, 'why are you growling at Sarah?'

He just whined again. I couldn't figure him out today.

'Anyway, the good news is, I'm getting you out of here.'

She pointed towards the exit I'd been heading for.

'You're *very* lucky,' she carried on. 'Very few people

ever get to use this exit.'

I was suddenly intrigued and I put my ghostlike stalker to the back of my mind. She was right; it was probably just a figment of my imagination anyway.

I scrambled to my feet. 'Where does it lead to?'

'Oh, you'll see,' she smiled, then headed off towards the exit I'd seen earlier.

'Come on, boy,' I said to Bandit, and trotted off after her.

He followed me, but didn't seem too enthusiastic. He hung back a bit, and checked behind him constantly. But he didn't make any noise and was heading in the right direction, so I decided to just let him follow.

As we got closer to the exit, I could see that it was a very old wooden door. It was firmly bolted shut... and padlocked.

'How are we going to get through that?' I asked.

It looked pretty impassable to me.

'I've got a key,' Sarah said, taking a huge, ancient-looking metal key from her pocket and fitting it in the lock.

Did SOE operatives have keys to all the doors leading from these tunnels? The huge key turned in the ancient padlock with a loud clunk. Within seconds, she had removed the padlock and pulled back the long bolts. The old door groaned as she turned the handle and swung it open.

'Wow - sounds like it hasn't been opened in years,' I said.

'Probably hasn't,' she replied.

'Why? Where does it lead?' I was really curious now.

'You'll see,' she whispered.

'Why are you whispering?' I asked.

'Shhhh!' She placed her finger over her lips.

I checked behind to see that Bandit was still with us. He was - his head still hanging a bit.

'Let's go,' she whispered, heading through the door.

I followed her, but she stopped just inside the doorway. She swiped at cobwebs and then coughed as the dust that had remained trapped in them for years filled the air.

'Stop hitting them,' I said, 'you're just making it worse.'

'What am I supposed to do then?' she spluttered.

'Here,' I said, showing her. 'Move your hand slowly, in a downward motion. That way the dust will just drift to the floor.'

She copied my movements, then turned to me and smiled. Geekpoints!

When we'd removed enough cobwebs to make out our surroundings, it seemed that we were in some kind of basement room, or cellar. Although the light from the HapHol device filled the room, it reflected off the cobwebs and didn't penetrate very far. I couldn't see the outer walls.

Sarah carried on moving into the room, feeling her way through the ghostly web.

'No one's been in here for a very, very long time,' she said.

'You'd be surprised how quickly arachnids can colonise an area like this,' I whispered, then winced. Why didn't I just say *spiders*? 'Although the dust does indicate that this place has remained undisturbed...'

Oh no - still sounding geeky! I decided it was probably

better for me to just keep schtum for a while.

We moved through the room in silence. Any sound we did make was dampened by the years of dust and cobwebs. It felt like we were walking through a vacuum, filled with the ghostly echoes of long-gone footsteps.

'We must be getting nearer to another wall,' said Sarah. 'There seems to be something dark up ahead.'

She quickened her pace and I slotted in behind her. I could sense Bandit just behind my heels. I reached down and patted his head. He'd been frightened back there in the tunnel and he was probably missing Aretha. The dog let out a soft moan.

Sarah had been right; we'd reached a wall. It seemed to be pretty solid and there were no openings or doorways, as far as I could make out. But at least it was a wall.

'We can follow this wall around,' Sarah said, patting it. 'We're bound to run into a door eventually.'

'Seems likely,' I smiled, following her as she headed off.

It went painfully slowly. This was a really big room but it wasn't empty. A few times, we had to make our way round old wooden shelving units, following them back to the wall before continuing. Finally, through the haze of cobwebs the outline of a door came into view.

'Let's hope it's unlocked,' said Sarah, ''cause I don't have a key to this one.'

I have to admit, I felt a tiny bit sick. I'd had enough of this dank cobweb-infested dust pit. But more than that - I really, really didn't want to have to go into those tunnels again. The thought of the darkness and the cold made my skin crawl, and I still had that gnawing feeling that someone or something had been chasing me in that tunnel.

'Oh no,' she said, banging her hand against the door.

'What is it?' I asked.

'It's got a keypad lock.'

'And?'

'And - I don't know the code.'

'Hmmm,' I said.

'What are you hmmming about?' Sarah asked.

'Gimme a minute,' I answered, pulling up my sleeve.

I flicked through some apps on my sWaP.

'No - not that one. Nah - too old...'

'What are you doing?' she asked.

'Wait, wait,' I said.

This might work. No! I needed a programmable keycard. Drat! Ooh - how about the one I'd been given by the guys who helped us get into CERN? I checked the code. No! No! No! Think harder, Renny...

'Aha!' I said. 'Gotcha!'

I remembered an app that Dragosh had sent me only last month. He'd stayed up for almost one week solid working on the algorithms. He'd been so hyped when he'd finally got it to work that he didn't even check the time before contacting me. It was 3 a.m. Even nerds like me are in bed at that time!

'How does it work?' Sarah asked, stepping back to let me get closer to the keypad.

'Well,' I began, then stopped myself, remembering the too-much-spider-info earlier on.

She didn't really want to know about the layers of coding. No one ever did. Just cut to the chase! I looked back at her. She was frowning.

'Um, it sort of listens for the right code. Kind of like

an old-fashioned safecracker. You know - three to the right, seven to the left...'

She nodded.

'Only this one sifts through billions of combinations per second.'

I have to admit that sometimes I am slightly jealous of Dragosh. He really is truly brilliant. Hope he doesn't end up straying to the dark side, though.

20

A soft clunk was the only signal we had that my app had worked. There were no red lights turning green or buzzing alarm noises. The magnetic lock just released itself once Dragosh's app stumbled upon the right combination.

I winked at Sarah, proud of myself. Well, proud that I knew people who could invent such things.

'Listen,' whispered Sarah, 'you need to stay back while I check it out. This place is very... um... well, let's just say they might not take too kindly to finding a couple of intruders running about.'

'But you have a key,' I said.

'I do, but this isn't exactly an authorised visit,' she whispered. 'When the abbey exit closed I had no choice. I couldn't take you out through the MI6 exit. There can be no links between you and any government agencies. The Westminster Abbey entrance was the best way to get you in and out. This option is the second best. But, believe me, it's not ideal.'

The look on her face was enough to stop my curiosity dead in its tracks. Wherever we were, it was clear that we weren't meant to be here. She didn't need to tell me twice. I wasn't too keen on getting caught by - well - anyone, really.

The dusty metallic doorknob squeaked softly as Sarah twisted it to the left. This part of the room wasn't as full of cobwebs as the rest. But it clearly hadn't been visited since this lock had been changed. And, judging by the lock's technology, that was probably more than ten years.

A sliver of light picked out the cobwebs on Sarah's hair as she gently pulled the door towards her. For just a second, she sparkled. Placing her foot in the crack, she flattened herself against the wall, right up against the doorjamb. Then, taking a deep breath, she peeked quickly around the doorframe.

She darted back inside, slowly breathing out.

'It looks clear,' she whispered.

'What's out there?' I asked.

'Looks like a disused corridor. We're still below ground level. No one's been down here in years, except maybe the occasional security guard doing a routine sweep.'

'Let's hope they're not doing a sweep today, then.'

I laughed nervously. Sarah smiled.

'Come on,' she whispered. 'Stay behind me.'

I followed her through the door and along the corridor. Why are the walls in these places always painted green? Had there been some kind of green paint surplus at some time in the past? There were a few other doors scattered here and there - all old, and all with similar locking mechanisms to the one we'd just left.

Right at the end of the corridor was a large, modern-looking emergency door. It was probably fireproof and alarmed. If I'd had to guess, I would have said that it led to the inside of somewhere. And since we were on the outside, I assumed that we needed to go through it and then find another exit - one that didn't lead to a dark tunnel.

Sarah's shoulders slumped as we got to the door.

'Another lock you don't have the key for?' I asked.

She nodded. 'And this one's probably alarmed.'

'Probably got a security camera on the other side too,' I added.

Sarah frowned.

'What?' I said. I was only trying to be realistic.

'Look, I'm going to have to call this in. I just don't think we can do this on our own. They'll have to extract you another way.'

'No!' I said firmly. 'I'll find a way.'

Sarah looked surprised. Oh no! What had I said? I was such an idiot. I'd been so keen to impress her that I'd just opened my mouth without thinking. Must remember to engage brain before opening mouth, Renny.

But I couldn't back down now. I couldn't just say, '*Oh sorry, moment of madness. I was just trying to impress you. You've got lovely eyes, and hair and...*'

To save face, I'd have to at least try to get us out of here. I needed to think. Come on brain. Think, think!

'OK,' I said, thinking out loud. 'The lock shouldn't be a problem. There's no reason Dragosh's app can't crack the code. And I don't see any biometric scanners, so we won't have to do a fingerprint or retinal scan.' I paused, thinking again. 'The only thing we really have to worry about is if there's an alarm...'

'And whether there are any security cameras on the

other side,' Sarah cut in.

'I may be able to do something about that,' I said.

I checked through my apps again. Recently, I had been given something that could send a particle scatter up to five metres. The particles created a kind of shield. It wasn't an invisibility cloak by any means, but any camera within range would be jammed. If anyone were watching, it would just go snowy for a while, then go back to normal once we'd passed.

'I don't even want to know where this came from,' said Sarah, once I'd explained my plan. 'Just - let's hope it works.'

I crossed my fingers behind my back.

Dragosh's app took a bit longer to crack the code for this door. Security was obviously tighter here. An orange light next to the key panel flashed and I held my breath waiting for alarm bells. Sarah gripped my arm and my heart pounded. It seemed very loud. Could she hear it?

I realised that I was swaying in time to the flashing of the light. When it stopped, I had to force myself to stand still. Could we go? Had Dragosh's app done it again? There was only one way to find out.

'Ready?' I asked, looking at Sarah.

Her face was serious, her brown eyes dark - intense. She didn't want to get caught.

'Yes,' she nodded.

I switched to the particle scatter app. As Sarah opened the door, I ran the app, then grabbed Bandit's collar.

'We need to stick close,' I whispered. 'This should only really be used for one soldier.'

'Soldier?' said Sarah.

Uh-oh, I'd let the cat out of the bag.

'It's kind of um... military,' I whispered, wincing. 'But I didn't steal it from the military. It's a prototype. Someone I know sort of develops stuff for them...'

Stop talking now, Renny. Just leave it at that. The military didn't want anyone to know about their collaborations with my friend Stingray. He's a brilliant developer but slightly loopy. Definitely not someone you take to meetings with you.

The corridor beyond was deserted. With the dim lighting and boring decoration this had the look of a service corridor. No top-level business execs ever visited this place.

Sarah followed me through the doorway in silence. I looked up. I'd been right; there was a security camera trained on the door. Luckily, it wasn't more than five metres away; otherwise, we'd have been spotted straight away.

Even though they couldn't see us, we crept cautiously along the corridor, like a couple of jewel thieves. I couldn't help imagining what might happen if an actual human being appeared. All the particle scatterers in the world wouldn't shield us then.

'Where should we head to?' I whispered, checking on Bandit. He was right behind me.

'Just keep moving,' replied Sarah. 'We'll have to play this by ear.'

We neared a bend in the corridor.

'Stop,' whispered Sarah, passing me.

This time she crouched down before peeping around the corner. She sprang back immediately, her face suddenly white. She raised her finger to her lips and pulled me down beside her. There must be someone around the corner.

I looked at Bandit, raising my finger to my lips. He bent his head low, his ears pricking up.

I looked at Sarah. Her eyes darted nervously up and down the corridor. She really didn't want to get caught. If we did, it would be a huge failure on her record. Never mind an embarrassment to her agency.

Seconds ticked by as we squatted, motionless. The dampening effect of the industrial carpet in the corridor meant we couldn't hear whether the person Sarah had seen was heading towards us. We could only wait, hoping they weren't.

The squeak of a swinging door made my heart pound even faster. Were they sending in reinforcements? Maybe my particle scatterer wasn't working.

I bit down on my lip. My leg muscles tensed as I crouched lower, ready to spring away from danger.

After waiting in total silence for a few seconds, Sarah sat forward, waving her hand in the direction of the squeaky door. She was going to take another look. I held my breath as she sprang forward, then darted back straight away.

'What?' I mouthed.

Smiling, she fell back against the wall, letting out the longest breath in history.

'Oh phew!' I whispered, joining her.

Bandit stayed perfectly still until I patted his head.

'Good boy,' I whispered. He wagged his tail happily.

After a few seconds, Sarah sat up. 'We've got to make a run for it, Renny. The longer we stick around, the more likely it is that we'll be spotted.'

'I agree,' I answered, although I wasn't exactly an expert on these things.

'I spotted a sign for the kitchen,' she continued. 'I think we should just make a dash for it and hope that we can get out that way.'

'OK,' I said, picking up Bandit. 'Just say when.'

'When!' she replied, grabbing my arm.

21

The walls of the corridor flew past in a blur. Sarah was able to drag me faster than I could actually run. My legs were finding it difficult to keep up. Mind you, I was carrying a fairly big dog under one arm.

Without stopping, she turned right, following the sign that showed the way to the kitchen.

We quickly reached the door marked 'Kitchen'. I crouched behind some wide green catering bins near the door, while Sarah peeped through the glass panel.

As I put Bandit down, I heard Sarah whisper something under her breath.

'What's wrong?' I asked.

'Staff,' she replied, pulling me past the door.

The next door was marked 'Laundry'.

'That's more like it,' she said, smiling.

She pushed the door open gently and checked inside.

'It's empty,' she whispered and all three of us darted inside.

Large carts of bedding and other laundry were scattered around the room. All the washers and dryers were busy. This was laundry on a big scale.

'Quick, put this on,' said Sarah, throwing a white

coat at me.

She pulled on something similar, then found matching hats. According to the badge on our coats, we were now proud members of 'Catering'.

'Excellent!' I said.

'A bit early to celebrate,' said Sarah. 'We're not out of here yet.' She grabbed my hand. 'Come on. And keep your head down. You're a bit on the young side to have a job here, so don't attract too much attention.'

'OK,' I whispered, lowering my head.

I wanted to ask where I was but she was pushing me towards the door. We left the laundry room and headed for the low, wide green bins outside the kitchen door.

Sarah grabbed one, opening the lid. 'Get in,' she whispered to Bandit.

He growled softly but did as he was told. We covered him with a couple of cardboard boxes. With as much confidence as I could muster, I followed Sarah into the kitchen, keeping my eyes down. She seemed to know where she was going. Maybe she'd been here before.

Large stainless steel preparation surfaces gleamed in the overhead lights. Chefs in white hats chopped and prepared food. Pots rattled and steam billowed from a large pan on a stove at the back.

With my head down to conceal my identity, we wheeled our bin through the kitchen, past all these busy people.

'Wait!' shouted a man at one of the food preparation areas.

I froze, not daring to look around. Seconds ticked by. I found I couldn't breathe. When I tried, my lungs just refused to expand. My body was going into full panic shutdown mode again. My vision started to blur. I could see a tunnel beginning to form. Oh no! Not now. This was really not the time.

'There's more over here,' said the owner of the voice, pointing at a small bin to the side of his table.

But my legs had frozen. I wasn't going to be able to respond.

'Cheers, mate,' said Sarah, stepping around me.

She picked up the smaller bin and emptied it into our larger one. Then, without even looking at me, she began dragging the heavy bin towards the door. It was made all the more heavy by the fact that I was attached to it, and she was having to pull me along as well.

'Renny,' she hissed. 'Move it - now!'

My right foot shuffled forward, then the left one followed. Reluctantly, my feet came back to life. Sarah's face looked a little less strained now. She was still having to drag the bin, but at least I was carrying myself.

As we crossed the long kitchen, I was only aware of the noise of pans crashing and people calling to each other. The stainless steel and chef's whites blurred as Sarah guided me across the kitchen towards the exit. We reached the door without attracting any more attention from the staff.

Sarah backed into the large exit door, using her body to swing it open. A gust of wind brushed my cheek as we carried on wheeling the large bin down a ramp into the back yard. The bin's plastic wheels trundled noisily off the ramp.

Sarah scanned the small cobblestone yard before turning to her left. My eyes followed hers. The yard was surrounded by high stone walls with a large gate set into the wall at the back. There was a bike parked against another wall, probably belonging to a member of the kitchen staff.

I noticed that the sky had darkened. It was nearly nightfall. We'd been in those tunnels longer than I'd thought.

'Over here,' she said, wheeling the bin around and parking it next to some others.

'Where are we?' I whispered.

'No time now, Renny,' she replied, grabbing my hand. 'Let's just get you out of here first.'

'What about Bandit?' I asked.

'He'll have to find his own way out,' she replied. 'We can't be seen with a dog.'

Sarah opened the lid. Bandit jumped out of the low bin and sniffed around the yard a bit. I bent down to make sure his tracker was working. It was.

'Go, boy,' I whispered.

He cocked his ears and headed off behind the bins.

'He'll catch up with us,' I said. 'If not, I'll find him.'

'He'll be fine, you'll see,' smiled Sarah.

We headed towards the large, solid metal gate at the back of the yard. This time we didn't need any apps or keys. Sarah drew back the long bolt and, after checking for movement outside, she pulled me through, shutting the gate behind us.

A chill breeze caught my hair, making me shiver. I shrugged it off.

I really needed to get in touch with the others. I pulled up my sleeve and was about to tap my sWaP's screen to call Iago, but Sarah stopped me.

'Not from here,' she whispered. 'We're not out yet!'

'What do you mean?' I asked, looking around.

We were outside the building now, in a small lane. Why weren't we in the clear?

'We're still inside a secured area,' she whispered. 'But don't worry - I can get us out.'

I followed her to the end of the lane. Then she stopped and turned to me, her face serious.

'Look, Renny, just do whatever I tell you to. And try to act natural, no matter how weird you feel. No panic attacks, OK?'

I nodded. I really needed to not mess up this time!

'OK, follow me,' she said.

She stepped boldly out of the lane, laughing quietly.

The short wide road was completely deserted. There were no cars parked anywhere and no people walking past, which is quite unusual for early evening in Central London.

'Yeah - did you see the look on her face... She looked like she was about to cry...'

Again, she laughed and I did my best to join in. Now I could see that we were heading towards a security gate. I could see one guard sitting inside. He was very still but looking in our direction. I hunched my shoulders a little, hoping he wouldn't look too closely at me in the fading light.

Sarah linked my arm in hers and carried on chattering about this made-up girl. The words just drifted past my ears. I had no idea what she was talking about.

'Renny,' she whispered, then laughed loudly. 'Act natural!'

'Oh,' I mumbled.

'Um - have you seen Richie lately?' I asked.

Did that sound all right?

'Not since Asha's party,' she replied. 'Maybe he's keeping a low profile after his body-popping routine. D'you remember it?'

She giggled, doing some arm waving. Now I did laugh naturally. She *did* look funny.

'Yeah. That was pretty embarrassing,' I laughed.

We were almost at the guard post by now. Sarah slung her arm around my shoulder and hugged me tightly.

'Night,' she shouted, waving to the guard.

He waved back and the security gate buzzed open.

'Keep moving,' she whispered as we walked through. 'Don't look back.'

The temptation to just glance over my shoulder was overwhelming as we walked away from the security checkpoint, but using all my willpower, I managed to control it.

'Turn left,' she whispered.

I couldn't resist a peek up at the road sign: Horse Guards Road. As we walked on, the impressive buildings to my left began to look very familiar. It was only when we crossed over the next street and I saw the familiar black railings that I realised exactly where we were.

'Sarah,' I gasped, 'were we just inside...'

I found that I couldn't finish my sentence. So many thoughts were whizzing through my head, the loudest of them shouting, 'Why didn't you pay more attention?'

She just nodded.

'I need to hear you say it.'

It was like it wasn't true until my ears heard it.

'Yes, Renny. You were just inside Downing Street!'

'Oh my word!' I whispered. 'No one's ever going to

believe me!'

I almost floated down King Charles Street and Whitehall towards Westminster tube station. It was only on the stairs down into the underground that I woke up.

'Bandit,' I said. 'I almost forgot. I'll check his tracker.'

'Do you need me to help you find him?' she asked.

I didn't really need her, but I'd kind of got used to having her around. I couldn't tell her that though, and I'd look pathetic if I said I needed her.

'No, no,' I laughed, waving my hand at her. 'I don't need you now. I'm sure you've got much better things to do than help a kid find a dog.'

'OK,' she said, tilting her head to one side. 'It's been fun, Renny.'

She smiled and leaning forward kissed me lightly on the cheek. Then she turned and walked away. I just stood there for a long time, staring. For all the heart-stopping moments, I'd really enjoyed our adventure together.

Bandit's tracking device pinged. I checked the map. He wasn't far.

I headed back up Bridge Street towards the junction with Whitehall, scanning the horizon for any sign of Aretha's dog. He wasn't moving, which was good, since although the area wasn't as crowded as it was during the day, there were still a lot of people about. It made spotting one dog more difficult than you'd imagine. And although the scanner was good, it wasn't pinpoint accurate.

Finally, I caught sight of him sitting outside a pub - St Steven's Tavern . He was casually glancing up and down the road, looking like a bored dog just waiting for its owner to finish his drink.

'Hey boy,' I said, patting his head, 'good escape. And your undercover work's not bad either.'

He answered me with a small woof, then stood up, his tail wagging with excitement. I actually think he'd enjoyed himself today.

'Come on, then,' I said, heading back towards the tube station.

As I walked back down Whitehall, I called Iago.

'Renny - where on earth have you been?' he asked.

'Sorry I've been incommunicado.'

'What do you mean, incommunicado?' he asked.

'I mean, I literally couldn't communicate,' I answered.

'Were you underground the whole time?'

'Not exactly,' I said and smiled.

Wait until they heard where I'd been.

'Listen Renny, just get here. A lot's happened since you left us and I can't discuss any of it over the phone.'

'Wow, sounds interesting,' I said. 'Any hints?'

'Well, let's just say that we need to make some fairly urgent travel plans,' he answered.

'Brilliant!' I said. 'See you in a while.'

We were off on an adventure and there was nothing I loved more. Well, as long as I had the rest of the ARCTIC6 to back me up.

22

Luckily there's a train from Victoria every fifteen minutes. Bandit and I jumped on the next one and were back home in less than an hour. I was starving by the time I'd walked from the station. By the look on Bandit's face, he was too. We headed straight for the fridge. I took out everything I thought I'd need and set it on the table. Then I filled up his bowl with goodies.

I was so hungry that I couldn't make up my mind what to put in my sandwich. After scratching my head a few times, I decided that everything went together, more or less. So I spread on the mayo and piled cheese, salami, ham, gherkins, lettuce and more cheese, then topped it all off with a dollop of coleslaw. I looked at it and grinned. It was truly a thing of beauty.

'What d'ya think, boy?' I asked Bandit.

He looked up from his bowl and growled. I think he liked it. I threw him a piece of salami as a reward. Before the meat hit the ground, he pounced and wolfed it down. He loves salami nearly as much as I do.

I'd just about got my chops around the mega sandwich when the kitchen door burst open.

'Put it down, Renny,' said Iago.

'No way,' I said, though my voice was muffled by the layers of meat, cheese and pickles in it.

'We need to talk,' he said.

'So talk,' I said, although it came out as 'nho nhalk'.

I think he understood me.

'We've received our travel plans...'

He frowned. This was getting serious. I took the sandwich out of my mouth. My stomach gurgled sadly.

'Where's Mum?' I asked.

'It's OK, she's upstairs,' he answered. 'We have a few minutes.'

'What are our travel plans?' I asked.

'Here,' he answered, sliding a large brown envelope along the table.

It didn't need to get very close before I could make out the logo. The deep blue globe with the red ribbon-like emblem across it is instantly familiar to everyone around the world. Well, everyone above the age of five anyway.

My hands shook as I reached inside. Why would we have an envelope from NASA?

'I can't believe it!' I gasped.

All thoughts of my adventure in Downing Street went flying out of my head.

'I knew you'd get over-excited,' Iago said.

'What's not to be excited about?' I asked. 'It's an invitation to Space Camp!'

I'd always dreamed of going there. Imagine - five days at NASA headquarters in Florida doing simulated shuttle launches and learning about space exploration!

'Renny,' he said, 'we won't actually be going to Space Camp.'

'Awwww,' I moaned, realising he was right.

The invitation was only a means of getting us to the US. But still, a tiny bit of me clung to the hope that when our mission was over, I'd get the chance to use the tickets.

'So,' I said, 'how did we get these?'

'Read the letter,' Iago replied.

I pulled out the folded letter that was underneath the tickets and read, 'Dear Mr Johnson and Miss Patterson, Congratulations! Your joint paper on kinetic energy conservation has been awarded the top prize by this year's Future British Scientists Council. The prize is a trip to NASA's space camp in Florida...'

I could feel the grin spread across my face.

'How cool is that!' I laughed, somehow proud that I might have written such a paper.

'You didn't actually write the paper, Renny!'

'I know,' I said.

'The prize includes flights and all expenses for the winner's plus one guest,' my cousin continued.

'When do we leave?' I asked.

'The flight's on Friday,' he replied.

'Great!' I said. 'Has anyone talked to Mum and Dad yet? What did your parents say?'

'They're quite happy,' he answered. 'With half-term coming up, that's us out of their hair.'

'I'm guessing you're coming to America with us. What about the others?'

'We told Silke about it. Not everything, just that we needed her help. She has invited the girls to go with her to Paris, just for a long weekend.'

'You're lucky to have an au pair with a flat in Paris,'

I said.

'I'm glad Dad met her father all those years ago,' he agreed. 'Silke's always there for us.'

It was true. Silke's father may have been super-rich but she wasn't snobby and she'd been really helpful in the past.

'And Cam?' I asked.

'He's going with the girls to Paris, then he's supposed to catch the train to Bordeaux. He's got some surf-buddies in the area. They'll meet with an SOE agent in Paris who will give them everything they need for their mission at the ITER site.'

'But these are all just cover stories, right?' I said.

'Yes,' said Iago.

'You know Renny,' my cousin sighed, 'this is all happening so fast, I've hardly had time to think things through.'

'We always operate like that,' I smiled. 'Hasn't done us any harm before!'

Iago frowned. 'I'd like to take five minutes to sit down and think about things this time, though!'

He was right. In the past, we hadn't had a choice. We'd just found ourselves in certain situations and had to react, or suffer the consequences.

'Renny?' called Tara from the hallway.

'In the kitchen,' I replied, before stuffing one quarter of my mega sandwich in my mouth.

'Your iPad was doing a song and dance,' she said, putting the gleaming device on the table in front of me.

'Hmmm mmm,' I said munching happily.

She smiled. I think she knew I meant 'thank you'. My sister and my cousin hovered around the table while I flicked through the applications on the screen. My iPad had been customised by a friend of mine. It could do a lot of cool things now, including act as a functional, if slightly big and clumsy, mobile phone.

There wasn't anything on the usual channels, no email or twitter message. Then I saw that one of my tech forums had received a posting in response to something I'd been chatting about with my geekfriends. But it wasn't from one of my friends. This was a new member, who'd only joined ten minutes ago. It might seem strange to post a message on a forum, but some of the ones where you have to register are more secure than an email account - more difficult to hack anyway.

I opened the thread, stuffing the rest of the sandwich in my mouth. I was expecting a cryptic message, but I was surprised that it was encrypted. Then I remembered Dragosh. He'd been suspicious earlier. Whoever was contacting me now obviously knew the capabilities of my 'friends'. They couldn't possibly post an unencrypted message. Even with the encryption, there was a good chance that Dragosh could crack it.

I downloaded the message and deleted the post from the forum. Most of my geekfriends wouldn't have seen it yet, but there was no way Dragosh would have missed it. He lived online - he was probably already running his best decryption software. And believe me, he had *the* best. But the sender would have known that. They'd have fitted a key that only I could know. So what did I know about that Dragosh didn't?

He knew pretty much everything I'd done as part of the ARCTIC6. It was difficult to cover our tracks. We'd had to reach out to a lot of people in the past.

The only thing he didn't know about me was what I'd been up to in the last few hours. But no one had given me anything and Sarah had taken the HapHol device back to SOE headquarters with her. So what could I possibly have that would decrypt this message? The only thing I'd had on me was my sWaP.

I looked down at my wrist. Could they have uploaded something while I'd been inside the building?

23

I pulled the stylus out of the watchstrap and tabbed through the applications on my sWaP.

I almost couldn't believe it when I saw it. But there it was before my eyes - a new application.

'What is it, Renny?' asked Iago.

'It looks like decryption software,' I replied.

'Where'd you get it from?'

'They must have uploaded it remotely.'

'When?' he asked, leaning closer.

'It must have been when we were inside the SOE building,' I said.

'That's like James Bond stuff,' gasped Tara.

I smiled, nodding my head. It felt good to be using Bond-like stuff. I pasted the message into a document and ran the decryption application.

'Renny,' said Tara as we waited for the decryption software to do its thing, 'where were you?'

'Oh... Downing Street,' I answered.

'What?' said Iago, coughing out the juice he'd been about to swallow.

'Sarah had to get me out through Downing Street.'

'No way!' said Tara. 'Did you see the Prime Minister?'

'No,' I laughed, 'all I saw was the kitchen.'

'Still... wow,' said Tara, smiling.

'Yeah, it was almost cool,' I answered.

The software had done its job. I could read the file. I leaned in closer.

'What's it say?' asked Iago, who was sitting opposite me.

'Both targets are go,' I whispered.

'Why are you whispering?' Iago asked.

'I just realised that Mum could be lurking around the corner. We don't want to give the game away.'

'True,' whispered Tara. 'It'd be stupid to get stopped by Mum, after all the effort the SOE has gone to.'

'Are there any more details?' asked Iago.

'We are to proceed with the authorised travel plans and they'll update us all once we're *in play.*'

'In play?' said Tara.

'You know,' I said. 'Once we're on our way.'

'Wish I was going with you,' she said. 'Your bit sounds much more exciting than mine.'

'Wasn't the last adventure exciting enough for you?' said Iago, smiling.

'Yeah,' she answered, 'I suppose so. I guess it's my turn to take a back seat this time.'

'I suppose we'd better go and pack our bags then,' smiled Iago, slapping the table.

He looked excited. And that made my heart race.

24

Florida
Friday 15th July

The plane journey was great. I'd never flown to the US before. It was strange to be travelling backwards through time zones - sort of like cheating time. Although my flight was around seven hours long, it would be only two hours later when I landed. I wondered what effect it would have on me. I did some internet research on jetlag and decided that the effects shouldn't be too bad, since I was travelling east to west and only crossing five time zones.

Our parents had been really great as usual. They trusted us to take care of ourselves. Iago and Charlie were old enough to fly by themselves, and besides, we were being met at the other side. The airline staff would take us directly from the plane to the NASA contact at the airport.

The staff took really good care of us, making sure we were comfortable and had enough to eat. Unlike most people, I like in-flight meals - all the little packages to open. I know it's all processed but it smells good when it's warming up. After I'd eaten everything offered to me - including the hot lunch option of chicken tikka masala and the chocolate pudding desert, I watched a film and dozed a bit.

I stepped out of the plane feeling refreshed and, if it's even possible, more excited than when I'd boarded. Charlie had been particularly quiet on the flight, but then Iago had been sitting between us so I couldn't exactly swap theories with her. We were escorted through passport control by one of the flight attendants - a lady called Julie. She then handed us over to a man from the airline's ground crew staff, who took us to wait for our luggage.

'You OK, Charl'?' I asked while we waited by the baggage carousel.

'Hmm,' she said. 'I'm just not sure about this, Renny. It feels wrong. We're usually the ones trying to stop the destruction, not cause it.'

'But this is different,' I said. 'At the moment all we know is that if they start up the LIFE and ITER machines there could be terrible consequences.'

'Yes, but surely there's a better way. You know... negotiation or something.'

'I'm sure they're trying all that, Charlie. You know we're just a back-up plan, in case the negotiations fail. We'd really be a last resort thing.'

She nodded, but she didn't look at me.

My phone rang. It was Cam.

'Hey, brother,' I said. 'You had time to do any surfing yet?'

'I'm still in Paris,' he answered.

'I know that,' I whispered, 'just trying to keep the

cover going.'

'Renny, I don't think anyone's earwigging on our conversation,' he replied.

'Oh, you never know,' I said. 'You just never know.'

'Anyway,' he carried on, 'just checking in. How are you guys doing? Any more information for us?'

'If you mean, did we hear from Professor you-know-who, then the answer's no. We're still very much *a go*.'

'Well, I've met with our contact here in Paris,' he said. 'The ITER machine is much smaller than the one at the NIF. There are also very few people around so we shouldn't have any problems. I'll keep checking in. Let me know if anything changes.'

As soon as we entered the arrivals lounge, I spotted a man holding up a card with my name on it. It was nice to be called Mr R. Johnson - made me feel important.

'There!' I said to the steward, who greeted our contact and checked his paperwork.

'Everything is in order,' he said. 'Enjoy your visit, guys.'

'Thanks, we will,' I called as he walked away.

Sadly, this was never on the cards. Mr Gibbons, the NASA driver, whisked us straight to our hotel, which was swankier than I expected. It had a gym, a swimming pool *and* a fancy looking restaurant. We'd have to spend the night in Florida and catch a connecting flight to California in the morning. We hadn't been able to take a direct flight, since our parents had to believe we were heading for NASA.

When I was finally alone in my room, I started to feel a bit down. I wasn't sure if it was because of the negative thing we were about to do, or just the fact that I'd come so close to going to Space Camp. I slumped down on the bed, all the adrenaline my body had produced used up.

The light knock at the door surprised me. I frowned, but stood up to answer it anyway. As I placed my hand on the door handle, an image of a man with a gun just waiting for me to open it flashed through my mind.

I shook the idea out of my head. *You're really getting paranoid Renny*, I told myself. No one, apart from the SOE, knew we were here and so far, we hadn't done anything.

'Who's there?' I asked through the locked door.

The knock came again. That was strange. Why wouldn't the person just identify themselves? A member of hotel staff would have done.

Once more, the person knocked softly. This time the knock was accompanied by a faint whisper.

'Renny - let me in.'

That wasn't the voice of a hired assassin. That was a soft, familiar voice. Not one I heard every day, but one I'd heard a lot recently.

'Sarah?' I whispered through the door. 'Is that you?'

'Yes,' she replied. 'Hurry up before someone sees me.'

I undid the lock as fast as my shaking hands would allow me to.

Sarah rushed in saying, 'Sorry if I made you worry, Renny. It's just that we can't be seen together.'

'Why are you here then?' I whispered.

'I'm your only contact with SOE, remember?' She held up a large bag. 'How did you think you were going to get your ordinance?'

I shut the door.

'I haven't got long, Renny,' she said, walking towards the bed. 'Mr Varken wanted me to explain everything to you, since you will be the one who completes the final part of the mission. You will have to give Iago and Charlie their instructions. OK?'

'OK,' I said.

She laid her bag down and unzipped it. I watched as she pulled out all manner of electrical cables, and what looked like timers and some small black boxes.

'Obviously,' she began, 'you won't be able to take any of this on the plane, but you need to familiarise yourself with the equipment you'll be using.'

'OK,' I said, nodding.

'Electromagnetic pulse devices,' she said, holding up one of the small black boxes. 'You know what an EMP does, don't you?'

'Yes,' I answered. 'I know they emit an electromagnetic pulse, which destroys any nearby electronic equipment.'

'OK,' she smiled, 'so all you have to do is enter your countdown and hit the "set" button.'

I gulped.

'What is it, Renny?'

'It just all seems so real now,' I replied.

'Look, all you have to do is plant the devices. They only destroy equipment –they won't hurt anyone. Besides, you know that this is a last resort. I'm absolutely one hundred per cent sure that we'll never need to press the button. OK?'

She spent the next half hour explaining the plan in detail, showing me where we'd need to place the devices, how to set the timers and the frequencies I'd need to create an uplink to SOE so that they could trigger the devices, if necessary. She also explained our cover story. We were to pose as students. There was a daily educational tour of the facility, so we would blend in.

After her briefing, I felt easier about our mission. After all, they weren't real bombs; no one was going to die in an explosion. They would just fry all the electronic equipment on the site, which would take years to replace. Our action would simply put the brakes on the scheme until the scientists and the government had a chance to check through everything properly.

'I have to go now,' said Sarah, repacking her bag. 'Everything you need will be on site when you get there. We'll send word as soon as you're inside.'

'How will you know when we're inside?' I asked.

She smiled. 'We uploaded tracker software onto all your phones while you were at the SOE building. I would have thought you'd have found it by now!'

I smiled. They were good. Then I frowned. Why hadn't I found it? *Starting to slip up, Renny!*

She headed for the door. 'I'll leave the blueprints of the building with you,' she said. 'You'll need to explain everything to the others.'

'Bye, Sarah,' I said, as she opened the door.

'See you on the other side, Renny.'

She winked then closed the door quietly behind her. I sort of missed her.

I called Iago first. He said he'd come straight away. He was a bit confused about why Sarah had come to me, since he was normally the leader. But I explained that some parts of the mission needed my particular computer skills.

Next, I dialled Charlie.

'What is it, Renny?' she answered, yawning.

'Did I wake you?'

'I was just reading and I must have dozed off. What time is it anyway?'

'Well, it's only five in the evening here, but it's night in the UK, so it's OK to feel tired. But listen, I need to talk to you. Can you come to my room? Iago's already on his way.'

'OK,' she said, yawning again. 'But I think I'm going to need some coffee or something.'

'I'll order it from room service,' I said, suddenly remembering that this was an all-expenses paid trip.

I had just finished ordering the coffee and some biscuits when Iago knocked on the door. He wanted to see the building schematics straight away, and we were busy working through the timings of each of our jobs by the time Charlie arrived.

'You *do* look tired,' I said.

'Thanks, Renny!'

She didn't look amused. Before she had time to shut the door, the coffee and biscuits arrived.

'Mmmm, smells so good,' said Charlie.

I poured three steaming cups of coffee and soon we were all munching on the biscuits. Just as we turned our attention back to the building plans, Charlie's phone rang.

'The number's withheld,' she said frowning. 'Should I answer it?'

Iago and I both nodded.

'Hello?' she said softly.

25

'It's Professor Green,' she whispered, covering the end of her phone.

Iago frowned. We went back to the paperwork while Charlie chatted.

'What did he say?' Iago asked as soon as Charlie hung up.

'He's still plodding through the science. There's so much conflicting data and he's having to go through everything by himself. Usually, he'd have a team of people working with him, but because of the secrecy, he's alone.'

'So why was he calling?' asked Iago.

'He wanted to ask us to wait for his call before arming the devices.'

'But he's not in charge, Charlie,' said Iago. 'Surely he should go through Varken?'

'Yes, but he doesn't know yet if there *is* a flaw in the scientists' calculations. We may end up destroying something that could take years to rebuild. And that would only happen if the public were willing to fork out billions of dollars.' She paced up and down. 'You know, it took years of funding and effort to get the programs to this point. I don't know if there will ever be the money or the will to do this in the future.'

Charlie's face was a bit pink after that speech.

'I think she's right,' I said. 'I think that no matter what orders we have, we should talk to Professor Green before we arm those devices.'

Iago was quiet for a while.

'OK,' he said finally, but he didn't sound convinced.

Charlie smiled and sat beside us.

'So - what do we have to do?'

We went over the plans again. I would be in charge of setting the timers on all the devices once we'd retrieved them, and all three of us would have to plant the devices in the target locations once they were set. Then I needed to get to a Wi-Fi location and create the uplink to the SOE. They would then be able to control the devices remotely. All we had to do, after that, was walk away. It sounded like a fairly simple plan on paper, but I knew from experience that getting into a facility, evading capture and locating a target was easier said than done.

'I'm starving,' said Charlie, standing up.

'Yeah, me too. When was the last time we ate?' I asked.

'On the plane,' she replied.

'If you don't count the whole packet of biscuits we just wolfed down,' laughed Iago.

'They don't count,' I said. 'We'll just skip starters.'

'Come on,' said Iago, putting his arms around both our shoulders. 'I'm sure this hotel's got a nice restaurant.'

'Ooooh,' said Charlie, 'do you think I can order the lobster?'

'Don't see why not,' replied Iago. 'We have to eat!'

We split up to get cleaned up and changed. I put on my one and only shirt and met the others by the lift. Charlie's blue dress shone in the mirrored wall of the lift as we travelled to the restaurant on the ground floor.

The lighting was low and soft music filtered through the chatter as the friendly waiter showed us to our table. This looked like a popular place to eat, with more than just the hotel's guests choosing to dine here.

We had the best feast imaginable. Charlie got her lobster. Iago had a massive steak and I had the tastiest spaghetti with clams I've ever eaten. When the waiter asked if we'd like the dessert menu, I almost said no. However, this was a once in a lifetime opportunity - shame to waste it.

Charlie sensibly went for the fresh fruit salad. Iago just had the trio of ice cream, but I ordered the double chocolate fudge brownie with whipped cream and ice cream on the side. Well - did you ever doubt that I would? I felt as stuffed as an over-filled pillow.

Although it was only 7 p.m., we were all really tired. It was after midnight UK time and besides, we had a flight at 8 a.m. to Oakland, California. With my belly aching, I said goodnight and went to my room. All I could do was lie on the bed and moan. This was never going to make me feel better, but I did it anyway.

A ping on my iPad forced me to sit up. I felt really unwell when I did.

'What?' I snapped at Dragosh's avatar.

'Hey - what has got into you?' asked Dragosh.

'Oh sorry! Too much pie,' I answered.

'Is that a crazy English metaphor for something, Renny?'

'Sadly, it's not a metaphor at all,' I laughed. 'I may not have had pie, but I had too much of everything else.'

'Where are you anyway?' asked Dragosh. 'You sound different.'

My ears pricked up instantly. Dragosh didn't mean that my voice sounded different. He meant that he could see that my VoIP pattern was different. The bits of information sending my voice over the internet were broken up and repackaged before Dragosh's computer received them. He had written a program that let him see the packages he was receiving. He could tell that the packages he was looking at right now were not the same as they usually were. It was his way of saying that he knew I was somewhere strange.

'Are you checking up on me?' I asked.

'No! Why? Have you got something to hide, Renny?'

My heart beat a bit faster. I inhaled deeply.

'Stop following me, Dragosh,' I said finally.

'Whatever,' he mumbled. 'But just so you know - I'm not the only shadow you've got!'

'What do you mean?' I asked.

'You've got a cybertail,' he said.

Then his avatar disappeared.

I felt rubbish. Dragosh had been a good friend of mine for years. Well, when I say friend, I mean geekfriend. We'd never actually met and probably never would, but he'd been there for me every time I'd ever needed his help. The trouble was, I couldn't let him in on this. This was a black op - something that the SOE could not be seen to involved with. It required complete and total secrecy. There was nothing I could do to fix the situation with Dragosh. I just couldn't tell him what was going on.

I don't know if it was that or my over-full belly, but I had real trouble sleeping. I spent the next few hours tossing and turning and had to get up twice for a drink.

When someone knocked on my door at 2 a.m., I had finally settled into a deep, happy sleep.

'Who is it?' I mumbled.

'It's me,' Iago answered. 'Let me in.'

I literally dragged myself out of bed and I had to cling to the door for support as I opened it. My eyes were still firmly shut. There was no way I was opening them until I absolutely had to.

'What happened to you?' asked Iago, stepping through the doorway.

'Couldn't sleep,' I replied.

'Well, you're doing a good impression of it now.'

'Ha ha!' I said.

I had to actually use my fingers to separate my eyelids. Even in the dim light of my hotel room, my eyes hurt.

'You not dressed yet?' said Charlie, entering my room.

'Not you too!' I moaned.

She ruffled my hair.

'C'mon, Rens,' she smiled. 'Let's get this show on the road.'

When I came out of the bathroom, showered and dressed and feeling slightly more human, Iago was on the phone.

'Who's he talking to?' I asked Charlie.

'Cam,' she replied. 'They're on their way to the ITER site; it's just outside Marseilles in the South of France.

They just got on the high-speed train from Paris. They have to change for a slower train for the last bit of the journey. But all seems to be going well. They're pretty resourceful.'

'That's good,' I replied. 'S'pose we need to get moving then!'

'That might be an idea,' she laughed. 'But not before we've had breakfast.'

'Oh,' I said, holding my stomach, 'I don't think I can.'

She smiled again. 'Just coffee then?'

'Yes please! Bucket loads of it!'

26

Livermere Centre, California
Saturday 16th July

After an entire pot of coffee, I returned to my room, stuffed everything I might need inside my backpack, then met the others in the lobby. Our taxi was waiting outside.

All the way to the airport, I kept thinking about what Dragosh had said. Why would someone be shadowing me? I mean, I could think of a thousand hackers and wannabegeeks who'd want to, but Dragosh wouldn't have bothered mentioning them. His filters could sift them out. If he'd found someone tracking me, then they must be pretty serious. I should ask him. But I couldn't right now. I didn't want to upset Charlie or Iago with what might just be a bit of geek-envy.

The domestic flight from Orlando to Oakland Airport left on time and was really more like a train journey than a flight, with no passport control or customs to go through. We touched down on time and were met at the airport by a car and driver. We'd heard nothing yet about where the EMP devices were hidden or how we'd get to them, but everything so far had been perfectly planned, so all we had to do was wait to hear from the SOE.

Charlie and Iago chatted quietly as we sped along the highway towards the Lawrence Livermore National Laboratory, where the NIF machine is housed. I spent my time going through the NIF's website, reminding myself of the science behind the experiments. It was amazing that they could create an actual 'Star on Earth'. By creating nuclear fusion they were able to mimic what happens inside the sun (on a much smaller scale, of course). I had to stop myself after a while though. My conscience got the better of me.

You see - I believe in all this. I'm a scientist at heart, and I think that we need to find new ways of producing energy if we're to survive. We can't just carry one burning up what we've got. Eventually we'll run out of coal and oil. And then what?

At the same time, I trusted Professor Green. If there was even a chance that there was an error in someone's calculations, then we should ask them to stop the experiment. And if they wouldn't see reason, then I understood that there had to be a back-up plan. I just didn't really like the buck stopping with me.

I still hadn't managed to put it out of my mind by the time we arrived at the NIF facility. *They're just EMP bombs*, I told myself as we walked up the steps to the reception area. *They might fry a few motherboards, but those things are all replaceable. Right?*

We walked across the open, airy lobby of the NIF facility.

'Welcome,' said a very pleasant receptionist. 'What can I do for you today?'

'Hello,' said Iago, 'we're here for the tour.'

'Oh, I see,' she smiled. 'Take a seat over there and your guide will be along shortly.'

I looked over to where she pointed. There were about ten other young people sitting around on the lobby couches, some chatting, others busy on their laptops. I was surprised. It was barely 8 a.m. These people were keen!

'Thank you,' said Charlie brightly, heading over towards the others.

There weren't any seats left, so the three of us stood by a pillar, waiting for our guide. I tried to eavesdrop on some of the conversations. From the snippets I heard, these sounded like my kind of people. One guy was talking about how he hoped to do his PhD here one day. I wanted to ask him what his speciality would be. Unfortunately, I needed to keep a really low profile, so I couldn't afford to get involved in any chatter.

'Follow me, guys,' came a man's voice from behind us.

I turned to look at him. He was quite young and wearing a white lab coat, which hung open. Probably a PhD student.

The other students all stood up eagerly, but Charlie, Iago and I hung back just a bit. We didn't want to get too involved in the tour. We'd need to sneak away eventually.

'Any news yet?' whispered Iago as we headed down the corridor towards the Visitors Centre, where they had scaled down models of the machines on site.

I shook my head, whispering, 'Sarah said she would contact us once we were inside the building and on the tour. She said they'd be monitoring us.'

My sWaP beeped. I tapped my Bluetooth and whispered, 'Yes?'

'Renny, it's me,' came Sarah's voice. 'Look, I know you can't talk, so just listen carefully. At the end of the corridor, you'll see the toilets. Make your excuses and leave the group. You'll find the third cubicle locked. You'll have to climb over from the next cubicle. The bag containing what you need is on the toilet seat. Set all the timers to five minutes. When you're ready, call Iago and Charlie. Distribute the EMP devices between you as agreed and get to work straight away. Call me when all the devices are in place. Is everything clear?'

'Yes, I whispered.

Charlie raised an eyebrow.

I nodded.

We were *in play*.

'Um, excuse me,' I said, pointing towards the toilets at the end of the corridor, my cheeks reddening in real embarrassment.

'OK,' smiled the guide. 'We're heading for the press room first, so you can catch up with us there.'

'Thanks,' I smiled and shuffled off.

I tried not to run but every now and then I had to hold myself back. Mustn't attract attention! The corridor seemed longer than it had done when I'd pointed towards the door. Every one of my footsteps echoed loudly. I slowed down, trying to walk more quietly. That only made the corridor seem longer.

By the time I reached the door, I'd chewed my lip so hard I could taste blood in my mouth. The door squeaked as I pushed it gently. The noise didn't end until I'd opened the door fully, and when I let it go, it swung shut with a louder, faster squeak. So much for not attracting attention.

There were six cubicles on each side. There was no one in the outer area, so I ducked down to check under the doors. No feet! All the other locks apart from the one on the third door were turned to the green vacant position. I headed straight for the cubicle next to it. The gap at the bottom of the partition wall was too small for me to squeeze through. I'd have to go over the top.

I stepped up onto the toilet seat, balancing myself. With my right hand I gripped the top of the partition between the two cubicles, then slipped my left hand over. I tried using my arm muscles to pull myself up. That was never going to work. I just ended up slithering back down to the floor. I climbed back up onto the toilet seat again. This time, I launched myself at the top of the wall. I managed to get my arms and upper body over the top, although it knocked the wind out of me. There would be a massive bruise when this was over.

Legs dangling like a puppet on a string, I grunted as I tried to hoist myself over the top of the wall. After three attempts, I finally managed to hoik my leg over. One final scrabble and my centre of gravity shifted from one side of the wall to the other. Now I had the opposite problem - how to stop myself crashing down on the other side.

I clung on by my fingertips, using my stomach muscles to try to slow my legs as they started dropping down the cubicle wall. I was starting to regret not doing more sit-ups. I didn't have much muscle there to call on. I tried to keep the noise down, but this was taking a lot of effort and the odd grunt escaped.

As I dangled there, I heard the sound that I had been dreading: the outer door began creaking. What was I going to do? I couldn't be caught here dangling between two cubicles. That would be the end of our entire operation. I had no choice; I had to drop and risk making a noise.

As the outer door opened wider, I launched myself onto the floor. The crash when I hit the floor and far wall at the same time was a lot louder than I'd bargained for. There was no way the squeak of the door could have masked it - could it?

'Hello?' came a surprised voice from the doorway.

They'd definitely heard me!

27

Now I panicked. Should I stay still and not answer? Maybe then they'd just go away. Drips of water splashed from a leaking tap, each one echoing quietly in the large room. What if it was a security guard or a member of staff? There was no way they'd just ignore me. No - I had to act.

'Hello,' came the man's voice again, closer now. 'Are you all right in there?'

'Um... hello,' I stuttered. 'I'm OK, just a bit queasy. Must be something I ate.'

'Did you fall? I heard a loud crash as I came in,' continued the voice.

'Oh no,' I replied, my brain whirring, 'I... I was just leaving - thought it was over - the um... you know. Had to make an emergency dash. Sorry to have troubled you.'

'No trouble at all. Do you need any help?' he asked.

'No, no, I'll be fine,' I replied. 'I think I'll just sit here a bit.'

'OK,' he answered. Then I heard the door of a cubicle on the opposite side of the white tiled room close and lock.

I sat there, heart pounding. Had he believed me?

Would he tell anyone? I waited for what seemed like ages, my breath coming in shallow gulps. How long was he going to take? Finally, the toilet flushed and I could hear him washing and drying his hands.

'You sure you're OK in there?' he asked as he passed my door.

'I'm fine, I'm fine,' I answered. 'Feeling a bit better now. Thanks.'

'OK,' he said, walking away.

A second later, I heard the door squeak again.

I let out a long sigh of relief. I couldn't risk any more interruptions to the plan. I needed to get the timers set and get back to the group before I was missed.

I unzipped the black holdall that had been left on the toilet seat. There were documents and maps inside, but I set to work on the timers first. If I didn't set them and get to the others on time, there'd be no need for the maps.

Setting fifteen timers with trembling fingers takes longer than you might think. Nervously, I checked my watch. I'd been gone ten minutes already. If I didn't hurry up, the guide would surely notice. That made my fingers tremble even more.

As I set the last one, the door squeaked again. Oh no! Not someone else to deal with.

'Renny,' whispered Iago as the outer door closed behind him.

I opened the cubicle door.

'What are you doing here?'

'The tour guide noticed that you were missing. I had to come and find you. I told him you hadn't been feeling well. What happened? What's taking so long?'

'Had a spot of bother,' I replied.

'Listen, we don't have time for explanations. We need to get going.'

'Just one more timer to set,' I replied, fumbling with the device.

Iago grabbed the bag and I stood up, stuffing the last device inside.

'Wait!' I whispered.

'What?' he snapped.

'We need to divide them up,' I replied.

'Oh,' he said inhaling deeply. 'Sorry Renny, I'm not thinking straight!'

Knowing that Iago was tense made me feel even more stressed. My cousin usually kept his cool under pressure. We could all rely on Iago.

He knelt down, placing the bag on the floor. He counted out my five devices, handed them to me, then counted out his own and placed them in his shoulder bag. I stuffed mine into my backpack, while he checked through the maps. Handing one with my name on to me, he zipped up the holdall.

'I'll just pass this to Charlie,' he said.

'OK. Ready?' I asked.

He nodded and I led the way out into the corridor.

'Cam called while you were gone,' whispered Iago. 'They've arrived at ITER and located their devices. It's only semi-operational so they only need three devices. Their contact was able to set the timers for them, so all they have to do is get them in place.'

'Sounds like a breeze,' I said.

'They have just as much chance of being caught as us, Renny,' he said.

He was right. None of this was easy.

When we rejoined the group, the guide asked if I was OK to continue.

'I'm fine,' I replied. 'I think it's over...'

'You look a bit pasty,' he replied. 'Let me know if you start to feel bad.'

I wasn't any pastier than usual, but I didn't want to tell him that.

'You OK, Renny?' smiled Charlie, draping her arm over my shoulder, dragging me away.

'Fine,' I smiled.

'All set?' she whispered.

I nodded.

Iago joined us, passing the bag to Charlie in one fluid move. She didn't even blink, just took it from him like a real pro.

We followed the tour guide for the next hour or so. The science was unbelievable. They'd even invented a way of cleaning up toxic nuclear waste. They could take spent fuel from nuclear reactors and use it to start the fission process. I was just starting to forget that we were on a mission when the guide announced a break. I checked my watch: 10.30 a.m. I tried to work out what time it was in the UK, but my brain was too tired to think.

'The restaurant's that way, and the nearest rest rooms are just down the hall. We'll meet back here in thirty minutes,' said the guide, before heading in the opposite direction.

'Let's go,' said Iago quietly as he passed me.

We headed towards the restaurant. Luckily, there was a huge outdoor eating area. After buying coffee and snacks, we made our way through the glass doors towards a picnic table under a tree. The facility was part of the larger Lawrence Livermore National Laboratory - a huge one-square-mile site with several other scientific research facilities.

'Are they set?' asked Charlie, swinging her leg over the attached bench.

'Yes,' I whispered, sitting down beside her.

Iago settled in opposite us.

'From what I've seen so far,' he continued, 'the map that I've got seems to be of that section of the building.'

He nodded his head, indicating a building behind us. I checked mine.

'Mine's that side,' I replied, nodding in the opposite direction.

Charlie frowned. 'Looks like I've got the rubbish job again - just like when I had to run miles through the underground tunnel at CERN.' She nodded her head to the left, indicating a building across the huge open space at the middle of the facility. 'Mine's way over there!'

'Mine's at the other end of my building, if that helps,' said Iago.

'Still a lot closer than mine...' replied Charlie, though she smiled.

'Mine's definitely the closest,' I added. 'Although we know there's a reason for that!'

'We haven't forgotten that you have to set up the link to the SOE,' Iago said.

'Hey! How you guys doin'?' came a voice from behind Iago.

I looked up, not knowing what to say.

'We're fine,' replied Charlie, covering my panic.

Meanwhile, Iago quietly folded his map and placing

it in his top pocket, turned around and stood up. Smiling openly, he offered his hand to the freckle-faced student.

'Hi! Nice to meet you. I'm...'

'James,' shouted Charlie.

Iago turned to her, frowning.

'And this is Edward,' she continued, pointing to me.

'And that's Grace,' added Iago, nodding towards Charlie.

'Oh, hi!' replied the student. 'I'm Kelvin. You guys are British, right?'

'Yes, we are,' said Iago.

'I'm planning on studying in Cambridge next year, so I just wanted to say hi.'

'Well, it's nice to meet you Kelvin,' said Iago, 'but we have to go and do something now.'

'Oh, OK. I didn't mean to disturb you,' replied Kelvin. 'Maybe catch you up later.'

I felt bad. He was just trying to be friendly. I watched him walk away, hands in pockets, head down.

'OK. Phones on silent?' Iago asked, as soon as Kelvin was far enough away.

We both nodded.

'Charlie, you go first.'

She stood up and walked away without glancing back at us. Iago's eyes followed her. I didn't turn around - best not to attract too much attention.

'You next,' said Iago, his voice cool now.

'You know where to meet up?' I asked.

'Course I do,' he replied. 'It's marked on the map.'

'See you there, then...'

I stood up and walked towards my target - the large building housing the LIFE machine. I hadn't walked twelve paces when my sWaP buzzed.

'Hello?' I said, tapping my Bluetooth.

'Keep in touch.' It was Iago.

'Will do,' I replied, and walked away feeling a bit more confident.

Head down, I made my way towards the massive building that housed the target chamber. The huge grey concrete building was the length of three football pitches. My instructions were to place my devices at various places in and around this building. I had what were labelled 'primary' locations. These were highlighted in red. There were also 'secondary' locations, coloured yellow. These were back-up targets in case I had any problems getting to the primary sites. We were doing all this in the middle of the facility's normal working day, so there were bound to be people around.

The door to the NIF building opened easily. I held my breath, then walked through it. I had to look confident, not suspicious. If anyone stopped me, I'd just say I was lost. But I really hoped no one would stop me.

I really didn't need anyone searching my backpack!

28

There was less noise in the massive square building than I'd imagined. Though that probably all changed when the giant lasers that fired the beam were running at full capacity. I sighed as I had another moment of regret. If my mission succeeded and if the scientists wouldn't back down, I'd be the one responsible for stopping all this amazing scientific work.

I needed to focus.

Quietly, I moved towards the back of the huge, empty space. The blue laser housing, covering the 192 laser beams, was made of polished steel. Each of these laser beams was focused by massive mirrors onto one spot on a concrete shield at the other end of the room. This shield covered the 'target chamber' - where the nuclear fission happened.

When I reached the back of the room, I took a breath, then peeped around towards the middle of the facility. There was no one in sight.

Walking quickly now, I made my way towards the first primary location– a junction on the laser housing with a control panel for one of the large mirrors. I opened my backpack and, like an experienced operative, attached the black device. The magnet attachment on the bottom of it clunked softly as it engaged. The whole thing took no more than ten seconds. Checking my map, I carried on towards the target chamber - the place where the 'Star on Earth' was created.

My second location was somewhere on the laser housing, near the target chamber. As I approached it, I looked around once, then took the device from my backpack and placed it where indicated. Again, the magnetic strip on the back of the device attached itself to the metal casing with a soft clunk.

My third location was almost directly opposite where I was, so I turned quickly, placed the device on target and checked my map. My final two locations were on the other side of the laser housing.

I ran back towards the other end of the room. As I reached halfway, I heard a door slam. Distant voices drifted towards me, echoing in the huge building. From the snippets of conversation I could hear, it sounded like the two technicians were headed my way. I turned my head frantically left to right. Where would I hide?

I spotted a small space under the massive metal tubing. I wasn't sure if I could fit in there though. Panicking, I turned a full 360 degrees looking for any other possible hiding place. There was nothing in here to hide behind. Apart from the long metal tubes covering the lasers and some access ladders, the building was empty.

The men's voices sounded a little farther away. This wasn't necessarily a good thing, though. The doorway was in the middle of the building. They'd have to walk to the end of the building in order to get around the laser housing, as I had done. As soon as they got around it, they'd see me.

I dived into the small space, pressing my back against the cold metal, drawing my knees up under my chin. I pulled my black backpack up in front of me, hoping that it might provide some cover. It wasn't much. If either of them looked down, I was a goner.

The men's voices became suddenly loud; they'd rounded the end of the laser housing. I'd only just missed being spotted. But I wasn't out of danger yet.

'See you in a minute,' said one of the men.

The technician's equipment jiggled about in his bag with every step he took, the sound growing louder the closer he got.

I gripped my legs tighter, trying to make myself as small as possible.

As the technician's shoe came into view, I shut my eyes.

I held my breath as he had passed me, stopping somewhere close by.

Whatever he was checking opened with a metallic ping. The technician dropped his bag of instruments on the floor. I could hear him picking through them, choosing the one he needed. He fiddled with something for a few seconds, then dropped something into his bag.

'All clear here, Jim,' he shouted. 'Just a bust screw. I've replaced it.'

Picking up his bag, he headed back past me.

I closed my eyes. *Don't look down. Don't look down.*

The footsteps grew fainter, then stopped.

The two technicians chatted again. I couldn't hear their conversation, but I wasn't really interested. I had other things on my mind.

My sWaP buzzed, tickling my wrist, and I checked the message. It was from Iago. All five of his devices were in place. He was heading back to rendezvous with the tour. I wondered how Charlie was doing. I decided not to message her. What if she were in a situation like this?

One of the men laughed and I heard footsteps. They were on the move again. I prayed that they were moving away from me. The voices grew fainter, as did the footsteps, until I could hear that they had turned the corner. I waited until I heard the outer door shut before I left my hidey-hole. Now I really had to get moving.

Throwing my backpack over my shoulder, I crept cautiously towards the end of the laser housing. As I turned the corner I checked the other side of the building. There was no one to be seen. I started running quietly. At the same time, I rifled through my backpack for the map. Slowing my pace slightly, I tried to focus on my next location - another junction on the metal tubing. I spotted it and had the EMP device out of my backpack before I reached it. I skidded to a halt and stuck it to the laser casing's metal frame.

While I was standing still, I checked the site of the next target. It wasn't far, but every footstep was taking me further away from the door. Picking up the backpack, I raced forward again, finding my final location. I breathed out heavily, as I put the last device in place. Now all I had to do was get out of here.

I'd be missed by the tour guide if I didn't show up soon. I'd have to run - take a chance that I was alone inside this building.

Stuffing the map back inside my backpack, I slung it

on my back. Then, taking several deep breaths, I began sprinting as fast as I could back towards the end of the laser room. My legs pumped harder than they've ever done before. The constant pounding in my ears drowned out the sound of my footsteps.

I didn't slow as I reached the end of the room; instead, I slammed against the wall, using it to change direction. An explosion of pain racked through my shoulder. But I had to ignore it; I needed to get out of this room.

Head down, I raced towards the other side, wiping the sweat from my forehead with my sleeve as I went. In a few paces, I rounded the other corner. The door was in sight. I was nearly free. Just a bit further.

My legs were starting to feel tired. I wasn't cut out for the 200-metre sprint. Each step was painful now. But I couldn't stop. I lurched forward, slowing with each step. Just three more paces.

A squeak - followed by a chink of light.

I juddered to a halt.

I was only one footstep away from the door.

The very air itself seemed to still.

29

As the door swung inwards, I darted behind it, flattening myself against the wall.

'And this, ladies and gentlemen, is where the magic happens. Just imagine - a 'Star on Earth'.'

It was the voice of the tour guide. The break was obviously over. Peeling myself off the wall, I slid out from behind the door. As the small group filed in, I joined on at the back.

'Renny,' whispered Iago, who was just stepping through the door.

Charlie was right behind him.

'All OK?' he asked.

I nodded in relief. The guide took us back up and down the now-familiar aisles of the laser room. I couldn't focus on what he was saying. My head was still spinning. I just drifted along with the group in silence until we got back to the door.

As we stepped out, Charlie said, 'Renny, are you OK?'

The fresh air made me feel a bit better. I ran my hands over my face a few times to snap myself out of it.

'I'm fine! Just had a close call. I'm so glad it was you

guys coming in that door.'

'Where to next?' asked Charlie.

'We need to get close to a Wi-Fi site, so I can create the uplink,' I said.

'Did they tell you where to go?' she asked.

'There's an empty storage room over that way, which backs onto a conference room with Wi-Fi,' I said, remembering the details from my map.

'Follow my lead,' whispered Iago.

We trailed along at the back of the group until they got back to the Visitor Centre. As the guide went through the door, Iago moved behind one of the large trees in the landscaped area in front of the building. Charlie and I stepped in just behind him. Once the tour group were inside the building, we began moving away. None of us looked back.

We crossed the open space between the buildings, trying not to attract attention. We didn't speak, just headed straight for the door of the storage room. With Charlie and I blocking him from view, Iago peeped inside.

'Seems empty,' he whispered, holding the door for Charlie and me.

There was very little in the room, just some shelving and bits of office furniture. I decided to set up in the farthest corner behind a row of empty shelves. It wasn't much cover, but it was the best I could find. Iago waited by the door in case anyone came near, and Charlie pulled her phone out of her pocket.

As I booted up my system, I glanced up. Charlie was walking over to Iago. I only had a glimpse of her face, but she was frowning. I couldn't hear the conversation;

their voices were too low, and besides, I was busy, but they looked serious.

Curious now, I stood up to see them better. Charlie was showing Iago her phone. His eyebrows shot up as he looked at it.

'What's going on?' I called.

'Charlie got a text message from Professor Green,' said Iago.

'And?'

'It says he doesn't think there's an error...' she said. 'It says we should stop what we're doing!'

'But why hasn't Varken contacted us then?' said Iago. 'He would have let us know if there was a change of plan. We can't abort the mission just because we get a *text* message telling us to. I mean - how do we even know that message actually came from Green?'

'It came from his phone number!' Charlie answered.

'Yes but you didn't speak to him, did you? Anyone could have his phone.'

'True,' I said.

'Oh come on!' said Charlie.

'Look,' said Iago, 'all I'm saying is that as far as we know Varken and Green are working together. We should carry on until we hear from Mr Varken.'

'No!' said Charlie. 'I don't agree. Professor Green wouldn't have sent me a message if it wasn't important.'

'Well, call him then,' said Iago. 'Get him on the phone and let us hear it straight from the horse's mouth.'

'I can't,' said Charlie. 'He's not answering.'

'There you go then!' said Iago. 'If it were that important, he'd pick up the phone, surely.'

'What if he can't? What if someone's stopping him?'

she answered.

'Now you're seeing conspiracies where there aren't any, said Iago, his voice growing louder. 'In any case, we're just here to place the devices and create the uplink. It's not like we have to actually blow the place up or anything.'

'But how do we know that Varken can be trusted?' replied Charlie angrily. 'What's to say he won't activate the devices after we've created the uplink?'

'OK. OK!' I said. 'You're making my head hurt! You can't carry on arguing like this. We're not getting anywhere. In fact, we'll probably get caught if you keep this up.'

They backed away from each other, but neither took their eyes off the other.

'Look,' I said, 'I see both your points of view. Iago, I understand that we've been given a mission and we don't know what's going on behind it. So your instinct is to trust the authorities.'

Iago nodded.

'And Charlie,' I continued, 'I get it that you trust Professor Green. To be honest, I trust him too. But Iago's right - we don't know whether the message you received is genuine or not. What if we're being fed false information by someone trying to derail our mission?'

'We go ahead!' said Iago.

'No! We do not!' shouted Charlie.

Oh no! This was like déjà vu. We couldn't keep going through this over and over again.

'Look,' I said, 'I've got an idea of how to solve our problem.'

'What's that, Renny?' snapped Iago.

'We ask for help.'

'How?'

'We ask the public to help us decide.'

'That's stupid,' said Charlie. 'This is supposed to be a black op. We can't ask the public.'

'I think we have to,' I said. 'Before we got that text from Professor Green, everything was black and white. But now I don't know if what the SOE are asking us to do is right or wrong.'

She nodded.

'I just think this is a decision that should be shared by as many people as possible. It's about the future of *all* of us.'

My voice cracked a bit at the end of that sentence. Charlie smiled.

'How are you going to tell the public?' asked Iago.

'I've got an idea,' I said.

My right eye winked all by itself. I flicked through the apps until I found the video record icon.

'Take my iPhone,' I said to Charlie.

She looked at me strangely but took the phone.

'Start recording me now, Charlie!'

30

'So - I think I've told them everything up to this point. Iago, Charlie - do you agree?'

'I think so,' nodded Charlie.

Iago just shrugged his shoulders.

'Then it's time for you two to take the stage.'

Iago stepped forward. Charlie held up the iPhone and continued filming.

'Those of you who've been with us for a while,' began Iago, 'will have seen or heard me do this kind of thing before. It's usually a life and death thing and you've always been there for me. This is a bit different. It's not actually an end of the world situation. But it could be!

'*If* the people who asked us to do this are right - and so far, nobody has *told* us otherwise, the errors in the scientists' calculations could be catastrophic. We *could* end up facing a scenario every bit as devastating as Killer Strangelets gobbling up matter, one atom at a time.'

Iago glanced up at Charlie, his eyes pleading. She looked away.

'So, basically what I'm saying is - we don't know what's going on. The only thing I *do* know is that if we don't do what we've been asked to, there could be terrible consequences. We are not being asked to make the hard choice whether or not to destroy these machines. We just have to create the uplink to the devices that will allow someone else to, *if* the time comes. It's a Plan B. It will only be used if all else fails.'

Iago breathed in deeply, then stared into the camera.

'You can't have a world where people can play with fire wherever they want to. If there's even the slightest chance that they could blow up the planet, there's got to be someone who can stop them! Don't you agree?'

He lowered his dark head and backed out of shot. I had to admit that my cousin was impressive. He just had a way about him. He was kind of strong and powerful, even when he spoke softly. I didn't fancy Charlie's chances.

She handed the iPhone to me.

'Are you going to introduce me?' asked Charlie quietly as she stepped in front of the camera.

'No,' I muttered.

'Oh! OK,' she said.

After a quick, shy smile, her face became serious.

'So,' she began, 'by now you know that my name is Charlie. And I'm not going to give you a big speech about the world and who controls it and who should be in control.'

Here she glanced at Iago.

'All I *am* going to tell you is that I trust Professor Green. He sent me that text - I know he did. And now I can't get in touch with him. Don't you think that's odd? Well - I do!'

She took a step closer to the camera, her blue eyes

flashing.

'I don't think we should hand over the power to cripple the facility that might be able to give us clean energy for the future. It could take years for them to get this place back up and running. In fact, it might never work again.

'Just imagine - if we do this. I mean, if we create the uplink and hand it over to Varken and his people, then we're responsible for whatever happens afterwards. If they *do* decide to activate the devices and destroy this facility, it'll be on our heads. Not just mine, Renny's, and Iago's, but yours too!

'If you're sitting at home wondering whether or not to vote, just imagine the future: a future without light and heat and power because we've used up all the coal and oil. Is this what you want for the future? Because, it's definitely NOT what I want.'

She lowered her head so that her hair fell forward. When she looked back up, her eyes were moist.

'We just need to wait a while...' she said softly. 'Just until we hear from Professor Green. Where's the harm in that?'

As she stepped away, I messaged B-Punk.

Geekboss: you get that?
B-Punk: loud &...
Geekboss: responses?
B-Punk: coming thru now

I switched apps on my phone. I hadn't had time to design something of my own, but I'd managed to find one that's ripped from some TV talent show. B-Punk was streaming live votes through it.

The two bars whizzed up and down as the votes came in. Sometimes Iago's red bar was highest, other times it was Charlie's green one. I switched back to my messaging app.

Geekboss: it's working
B-Punk: how long you need?
Geekboss: 10 mins

I was just about to switch back when my iPad beeped. I recognised the beep this time.

'Dragosh,' I said when his avatar popped up.

'This you, Renny?' he asked.

'What?' I replied.

'Oh don't try to dance with me, Renny. I know all your moves.'

'OK, it *is* me.'

There was no point in denying it.

'Why didn't you come to me?' he asked.

'Look, no offence, Dragosh, but B-Punk has certain skills in this area. I'm not saying he's better, but he's the best in gamerland.'

'True, I suppose...' muttered Dragosh. 'If I needed anyone, he'd be my first choice too.'

Now it was my turn to feel insulted.

'You need anything from me?' he asked.

I thought about it for a moment. There wasn't anything Dragosh could do for me right now, but he was a really handy friend to have and some day when he needed my help, I'd like to think he'd want me around.

'Tell you what,' I said, 'stick around a bit. I'll let you know.'

'OK,' said Dragosh.

I couldn't see him, but he sounded like he was smiling.

I checked the phone app again; the vote was going in favour of Charlie now. She had been pretty amazing, even better than Iago. But this wasn't a popularity contest. I thought about what Charlie had said about Professor Green's text. Even though we'd been asked to do this by a government department, I was starting to believe that they were wrong - that this wasn't the right way to solve their problem.

Still, I would respect the public vote. Many minds are usually better than one. The people I'd reached out to may not have exactly been Joe Bloggs, but they were a pretty smart lot and I'd relied on them before.

I checked my message app. I had one.

B-Punk: 2 mins more

Geekboss: 2 the wire

B-Punk: understood

I wasn't going to shut this vote down even one second early. Every vote counted. I checked the counter. Iago was fighting back. People were probably replaying both speeches over and over before deciding.

My sWaP wrist phone rang. It was my brother. I tapped the Bluetooth earpiece.

'Cam,' I gasped. 'Am I glad to hear from you.'

'What's happening, Renny?'

'Where've you been?' I asked.

'In bed! It's the middle of the night here,' he answered.

'Oh,' I said, my brain unable to do the calculation.

No wonder though. My body must have been going through all kinds of tiredness.

As I explained the situation to my brother, my thoughts were in overdrive. Why had I felt so uneasy in the SOE office? And why was Dragosh convinced I had a cybertail?

'There's nothing we can do here,' said Cam. 'The devices are in place and even if we wanted, we couldn't get them out until tomorrow.'

'I know,' I answered.

'Just do the right thing, Renny,' my brother said.

Then he was gone. Dragosh beeped me on my iPad.

'For what it's worth,' he said, 'I voted for Charlie... and not for the reason you're thinking.'

I smiled.

'There have been many horrors created in the name of science,' he continued. 'Diseases that were invented to kill off animal "plagues"...'

I knew what he meant. Diseases like myxomatosis had been introduced into the rabbit population to keep their numbers down. The results were horrible - the animals suffered terribly. This was not a humane way of dealing with overpopulation.

'Then there was DDT,' he said.

'I remember hearing about that,' I answered. 'It was a fertiliser that caused cancers. Wasn't it?'

Yes, he replied, 'but worst of all was the atom bomb and its hideous offspring: the nuclear bomb.'

He stopped for a moment, gathering his thoughts.

'But we can't stop science. There always has to be a hope that one day their work will be used for the good of everyone and everything on the planet. At least that's what I hope!'

'Me too, my friend,' I said. 'Me too!'

I smiled. Maybe I shouldn't have been so wary of Dragosh in the past. At the same time, I knew we were all geeks together. We would probably end up suing one another for stealing the other's ideas when we were older. Isn't that what all geeks do?

'Hold on just a second, Dragosh,' I said, checking the iPhone, 'I've got a message coming in.'

B-Punk: Lines closed

Geekboss: Thnk u

This was the moment of truth.

'Iago, Charlie, come here,' I said.

They moved slowly towards me, neither looking at the other.

'You both promise that no matter what the vote, you'll go along with it?'

They took their time nodding, first Charlie and then Iago. I held up the iPhone for them to see. The results were clear.

Charlie looked down, breathing out slowly.

31

'Suppose that's it then,' said Iago bitterly.

'Don't be like that,' said Charlie. 'This didn't have anything to do with you and me. This was people voting for the future - our future.'

'Look,' said Iago, a bit more gently, 'do whatever you think is right, but I'm not going to be the one who has to tell them.'

Oh, I hadn't thought about that! Someone had to do the deed. Charlie looked at me.

'Aww no!' I said. 'Why does it have to be me?'

'It was your idea,' said Iago.

'S'pose it was,' I replied.

I'd got us all into this. I'd have to be the one to make the call. But this was a black op, completely off the record. We didn't exactly have Varken's direct line. He had been clear. There could be no direct communication between him and us in case we were caught.

'Dragosh?' I said, flicking through the open files on my iPad.

True to his word, he was hanging around.

'Dragosh, I need your help.'

'What is it?'

'I need to find someone's phone number. And as you can see, I haven't got access to my usual resources.'

'No problem,' replied Dragosh. 'Where do you want me to look?'

'Well, that might be tricky,' I said. 'She works for a government agency that technically doesn't exist.'

'Oh, you mean the girl who came to your hotel yesterday?'

'Yes,' I replied, more than a little bit surprised. 'How did you know about her?'

'Oh, Renny, you don't think I didn't know where you were, do you? I followed your IP. You've got some good decoys in place but in the end I found you.'

He was right. I had set up a system that bounced my IP address around the globe a few times. This put most people off my trail, but anyone serious would eventually be able to figure out where I was working from.

'So how do you know about Sarah?' I asked.

It was one thing being able to locate my computer but this was something else.

'It really wasn't so difficult to get into the hotel's CCTV system. And you know the best part?'

'What's that?' I asked.

'I used *your* face-recognition software to ID her.'

'No way!'

'Seriously,' he continued. 'And considering she's an operative, she was pretty easy to find.'

'What do you mean?'

'Oh, they'd wiped everything, you know - all her social network info and postings. But only on the surface. I was able to go back and dig around.'

I knew what he meant - the trouble with information

on the net is it's never really deleted. When you delete something, all you're actually doing is breaking up the links between the bits of information. The actual information itself doesn't really go away. Someone with the time and ability can basically undelete stuff.

'Anyway, you want her number or not?'

His avatar was bouncing up and down, holding its belly as Dragosh chuckled.

'Yes, of course,' I said. 'But stick around.'

'I'm here - like something smelly,' he answered.

I dialled the number Dragosh had given me straight away. A man's voice answered.

'Hello,' I said.

'Who is this?' he asked. He sounded annoyed.

'May I speak with Sarah please?'

I wasn't about to be put off now. I heard some shuffling noises, then a female voice came on the line.

'Hello, who is this?'

She sounded more concerned than annoyed.

'It's Renny,' I said.

'What? How did you get this number?'

Now she sounded flabbergasted.

'I have... friends,' I replied.

'Why are you calling, Renny?'

'We wanted to tell you, well Mr Varken actually, that we don't want to go ahead with the uplink. We've had a message from Professor Green. He thinks there's nothing wrong with the scientists' work. And we want to wait until we hear more from him. We don't believe there's going to be a supernova... a Killer Star.'

I felt good. I felt strong. I'd said my piece.

There was silence on the other end of the line.

'Sarah... are you still there?' I asked.

I heard a click, then the line went dead.

'What's happening, Renny?' asked Iago.

'The line just went dead,' I answered.

'I suppose that's it then. We're dismissed. Let's pack up and get out of here,' said my cousin, picking up his bag.

'Don't you think it's strange that she just hung up?' said Charlie. 'I mean, I understand that she was probably disappointed in us, after all she did to make this happen. But still...'

Charlie shook her head and walked over to pick up her bag.

'Well, I suppose it doesn't really matter,' I said. 'They won't be able to activate the devices without the uplink.'

Iago was shaking his head.

'I just don't know if we did the right thing,' he said.

I was starting to feel a bit guilty that we'd let down the people at the SOE. They did have a very good argument. What if they were right and the star could supernova? So far, all we had against them was a text from Professor Green.

I argued with myself while I shut down my laptop and began packing away my things.

I stood up to join Iago and Charlie, who were waiting in silence, when the door burst open. Four large men, dressed in black from head to toe, raced through the door. Not that I would have tried to do anything, but the huge black rifles they trained on us had the desired effect.

'Drop the backpack,' shouted the one nearest to me.

The backpack hit the ground before he'd finished the

sentence.

'On your knees,' he commanded, 'hands behind your head.'

I dropped and did as I was told.

I looked around. Charlie and Iago were in similar positions.

One of the other men rushed forward, grabbing my bag and handing it back to the man nearest me, who was clearly the leader.

He rifled through it, pulling out my laptop.

Kneeling quickly, he opened the laptop and started it up.

Oh no! I hadn't had time to dump anything. If he could figure out my password he'd have instant access to the uplink.

'Why are you doing this?' I asked feebly.

The man looked away from the screen. 'We never really trusted you to go through with this. The truth is, we only needed you to plant the devices. We'd never have been able to get three adult operatives in there unnoticed. But now that you've planted them, it's just a question of establishing the uplink. You must realise that we can do that without you.'

He was right. We'd done the only bit that they couldn't do. Anyone could hide out in an abandoned storeroom and create a satellite uplink to London.

'Give me your password or you'll regret it,' he said.

His voice was level and calm, but scary all the same.

When I didn't respond, he waved one of his men towards me.

As the man got closer, I felt my clammy hands sticking to my neck. I tried to swallow but my mouth had suddenly dried out.

Casually, but with incredible speed, the man planted the point of the gun's barrel onto my right temple.

My heart skipped a beat. Then it did a funny double beat, which hurt.

'Tell me the password,' shouted the leader.

The gun pressed harder against my head.

I wanted to shout 'no', but then I remembered something Varken had said about SOE using freelancers. These men were mercenaries. They were doing this job for money and they wouldn't get paid if they didn't create the uplink. There was no telling what they'd do to me to get that password.

'Try UDFY-38135539,' Charlie blurted out.

I looked around at her, my mouth falling open. How did she know my password?

'Sorry Renny,' she said, lowering her gaze, 'I can't let them hurt you.'

'But how did you know it?' I asked.

'I remember last year that you were totally amazed at the images from the Hubble Telescope of the oldest galaxy ever seen. You couldn't stop saying its name. It just stuck in my head.'

'Mine too!' I said, shaking my head sadly.

Now they had the password, there was nothing I could do.

The head mercenary entered my password and found my files with no trouble whatsoever.

'All set,' he said, picking up my laptop and turning to his men. 'Let's go.'

That was it - the devices were armed

32

The men backed out of the room, their weapons trained on us until they'd reached the door.

'Don't go anywhere now,' chuckled their leader.

My lip curled.

He slammed the door roughly, then I heard something rattle against it.

Iago ran towards the door pushing at it.

'He's blocked it with something,' my cousin said, banging his fist against the door.

'I'm sure they'll send someone to get us eventually,' said Charlie, sitting down on the floor.

My phone rang.

'Yeah?' I answered.

I sounded as down as I felt.

'Renny, it's Sarah.'

'Calling to gloat?'

She didn't answer.

'Look, Sarah, whatever it is, I don't want to hear it. It's been a long couple of days and since you obviously don't need us any more, we'd like to go home. OK?'

'Um... Renny,' she continued, 'I... I don't know how to tell you this...'

'Tell me what?'

She was starting to annoy me now. If she had something to tell me why not just *tell* me?

'Put me on speakerphone, Renny.'

I did so and called the others closer.

'I just found this out...' she said. 'You've got to believe me. I would never have gone along with this if I'd known.'

'If you'd known what?' asked Iago.

'That the bombs aren't just EMPs,' she replied.

'What are they then?' I asked.

'They're also filled with a highly explosive substance. Varken just told me that the plan is to blow up the facility so that it's beyond fixing.'

My stomach heaved.

'But why would he do that?' I asked, fighting to control my feelings.

'When I called him just now he said he couldn't tell me. That I wasn't to question his orders, just do as I was told. I... I'm not sure,' she said, 'but I suppose he could be doing this for money.'

'But who would be paying him?' asked Charlie.

'I can only guess,' I said, 'but I suppose if you owned a coal mine or an electricity company, you wouldn't really want anyone to develop another power source, especially not if it was clean and the supply was endless.'

There were plenty of people out there with motive.

'Then we have to go back,' said Iago, jumping to his feet.

'And do what?' asked Charlie. 'The timers have been set. We can't unset them. Once they're activated we've only got ten minutes.'

She was right.

'Then we'll have to get them out of there,' said Iago.

'But where will we put them?' I asked.

'It doesn't really matter,' he answered, 'so long as they aren't anywhere near the LIFE machine.'

'But the bombs will still go off!' I said.

'Yes, but we can call security - get them to evacuate the facility...' He shook his head. 'Anyway, I can't think of a better plan right now. Can you?'

'No,' I answered, shaking mine.

'Me neither,' said Charlie.

'I'm sorry,' said Iago and kissed Charlie lightly on the forehead. 'You were right - we should have listened to Professor Green.'

'It's OK, we were all confused,' she said. 'Let's just try to make this right.'

'OK then,' said my cousin. 'We each go back and get the devices we planted and bring them here. Agreed?'

'But we need to get out of here first,' I said.

'I'll call security,' said Iago, fishing out his phone.

'Wait a minute... wait a minute,' came Sarah's voice from my phone. 'If you call security they'll arrest you. I mean, look at your situation...'

I looked around at the others. She was right. If we told them that we'd planted bombs on this facility they'd have us arrested straight away. There was no way we'd get to the devices then.

'We've got to get to the devices first, then call security,' said Iago.

'Sarah, we'll call you back,' I said, ending the call.

'But how do we get out of here?' said Charlie. 'They've barricaded the door and I can't see any windows.'

I looked around frantically. *Think, Renny - there must be something.*

'Air!' I said.

'What?' said both Iago and Charlie in unison.

'There are no windows in here, so the air has to come from somewhere.'

I raced to the nearest wall, turning my face upwards; air vents were usually high up, near the ceiling.

'No. No. No,' I said, moving along the wall carefully. 'Come on, you two. Don't just stand there!'

Charlie ran to one side of the room, Iago the other. We all moved in total silence along the walls.

'Here! Here!' shouted Charlie, waving her arm.

Iago and I ran to where she'd stopped. Sure enough, at the top of the wall was a small grille. I could feel the cool air spilling through it, even from down here. Iago pulled out his camping multi-tool.

'One of you will have to unscrew it,' he said. 'You'll have to stand on my shoulders.'

'I'll do it,' I volunteered. 'I'd rather be doing something than standing around thinking.'

Iago selected the Phillips screwdriver, then put out his knee for me to stand on. As Charlie helped me to climb onto his shoulders, I tried not to think about the timers and how long we had left. Better to just keep working.

The first and second screws came away easily enough, but the bottom left one was stuck and I had to use both my hands to get it to budge. Finally it moved and the grille swung free, attached now by only one screw, which I didn't need to bother with. I could see the hazy blue sky through the hole in the wall.

'Who's going in?' I asked, looking down at my

cousin.

'You,' grunted my cousin, straining to support my weight.

'Why?' I asked. I didn't fancy crawling through a tiny air vent.

'You're the smallest,' he answered.

I couldn't argue with that.

'Come here, Charlie,' said Iago. 'Grab his foot.'

I could feel Charlie guiding my foot onto her shoulder.

'OK, PUSH!' shouted Iago.

I shot upwards so suddenly I wasn't prepared. Luckily, I scrabbled for the opening as my body fell back downwards. When my hands grasped the lower edge of the opening I pulled myself forward. At the same time, I felt Iago and Charlie push my feet again.

I hurtled head first through the air vent, stopping only when my belly caught on the edge of the hole in the wall. I was half-in, half-out now. I twisted myself around so that I could get into a sitting position.

A low roof edge was just within my grasp. Reaching up, I grabbed hold of it, hauling myself upwards so that I could get my legs through the air vent.

Now I was dangling like a rag doll from the roof. I looked down. It wasn't a very long drop - probably not more than six feet - but it was onto hard concrete.

Reluctantly, I let go.

The jarring pain didn't come as a surprise, but it still hurt. I gripped my knee, rolling on the ground for a few seconds. I had to bite my lip to keep from crying out.

Eventually the pain dimmed a bit and I was able to stand up. I limped miserably around the side of the building to the door, which it turned out wasn't barricaded. A metal bar had been jammed between the handle and the wall, acting like a bolt. If we'd known, we would have probably been able to dislodge it by ramming it from inside. It would have saved us some time.

And time was something we were running out of...

33

'Let's go,' I shouted, pulling the door open.

'As soon as I've got the devices out, I'm calling security,' said Iago. 'Even if you two haven't got back to me. All right?'

'Yes,' nodded Charlie.

Agreed,' I said.

'Good luck,' said Iago, clapping me on the shoulder. Then he turned to Charlie, enveloping her in his arms.

They pulled apart and started running towards their locations, just as I headed off. As I ran, I thought about calling Cam, but there was no point. They'd never get to the devices in time. They were probably hours away by now. The facility at ITER would probably be destroyed, but we could still try to save the technology here. At least Cam, Tara and Aretha were safe!

The building housing the ignition chamber seemed further away than it had a minute ago. I kept on going, my mind processing what Sarah had said. I'd come across greedy people before, so easily swayed by the sight of money. Still, I would have thought that the head of a government agency would've had a bit more conscience.

Things began to come back to me as I hurtled towards

the building: the creepy outline of the man in Varken's office, Bandit's strange behaviour, the feeling that I was being followed in the tunnel, and the cybertail on my computer that Dragosh had mentioned. Maybe Varken wasn't all to blame.

I called Sarah as I ran.

'Sarah,' I shouted into my Bluetooth earpiece, 'does this seem out of character for Varken? I mean - do you think anyone else at the SOE is involved?'

'Well,' she answered, 'he's had an impeccable career to date. But I suppose you never really know someone, do you?'

'No,' I said, 'what I mean is; has anyone been behaving unusually? Like one of your colleagues.'

'All my colleagues have been normal,' she answered. 'But I never liked Mr Tourdeville...'

'Who is Mr Tourdeville?' I cut in.

'He's a security consultant. He only joined us last month. But he ordered me to do things I didn't agree with.'

'Such as?'

'He was following us when we were in the tunnel. When I asked him why, he mumbled something about keeping tabs. When I told him you were still down there, he said I had to get you out without you seeing him. He's the one who gave me that key - the one that got us into Downing Street. He said it was better that you didn't know about him.'

'I didn't really get a good look at him,' I said. 'The room was too dark. What does he look like?'

Suddenly all my feelings and worries of the last few days came flooding back; the uneasy feeling I'd had at the SOE and Dragosh's cybertail. I wasn't going to jump to any conclusions just yet but this was all starting to come together... horribly, scarily together.

'Well, he's normal height and build, but there is one remarkable thing about him.'

'What's that?' I asked.

'His teeth - he has these gleaming white over-perfect teeth. They kind of have a life of their own, if you know what I mean.'

'Sort of Hollywood White?' I asked, panting as I ran.

'Yeah,' she laughed slightly. 'That's a really good description, Renny. It's almost as if you'd seen him before.'

'Oh, I have,' I announced, the sweat pouring down my body turning suddenly cold.

'What do you mean?'

She sounded worried.

'I mean the man you've been working with for the last month is Peter Gek!' I stopped, the stitch in my side becoming unbearable. 'He's the man who tried to murder the US President last year...'

'What?' she almost screamed. 'But we've got pictures of him. This isn't the same man.'

'Sarah, it's pretty easy to change your face if you've got the money,' I replied.

'But why didn't he change his teeth?' she asked.

'Vanity,' I answered, 'he *loves* those teeth!'

I reached the door to the laser room.

'Sarah, I've got to go.'

'OK, one last thing though, Renny - why would Varken go along with him? Planting EMP devices to stop scientists from doing something dangerous is one thing... but sending in those mercenaries, knowing the bombs could kill people, doesn't sound like him.'

'Does Varken have a family?' I asked.

'Yes,' she replied slowly.

'Sarah, get the police over to Varken's house.'

'Do you think Gek's holding them captive?' she asked.

'I've seen him do worse!'

Hanging up, I flung the door back. I didn't care now who heard me and whether there was anyone inside. With my heart in my mouth, I bolted down the long structure towards the end of the laser housing. The lights above me flashed brighter then dimmed as I passed under each one. I found myself counting their dim reflections in the blue laser housing.

Blood pounded in my temples as I reached the corner. Each beat marked a second ticking by. I wondered how much time I had left.

Again, I slammed against the wall, using the force of the collision to turn the corner. I raced up between the tunnel's two long laser arms, easily finding the first device I'd planted. I barely slowed down as I grabbed it. My legs were moving faster than they'd ever done before. The blue paint of the laser casing whizzed past, only the odd feature now catching my attention.

I reached the second device, grabbed it, then raced forward to detach the third device from near the ignition chamber. I only needed to grab it and then start my dash around the other side of the huge laser casing.

My fingers locked around it and I turned my body away to pull it free. But it wouldn't budge. I stopped dead in my tracks. Maybe I hadn't pulled hard enough.

I tightened my grip on it, planted my feet, and pulled again, this time with all my might.

No go! It wouldn't budge.

What was I going to do? The magnetic strip on this one must have been stronger than the others. I had nothing to lever it with. But more to the point, there were two more devices to be removed. I made a split-second decision. I couldn't just stand here like a lemon with the two devices in my hand, trying to remove the third one.

I raced back towards the end of the building. I'd get the other two devices and get out of here. Then I'd go back for the last one. That was my only choice. Otherwise, all five devices would end up going off more or less where Gek had intended.

I found the other two devices and they came away easily enough. With my heart muscle actually hurting because my blood was pumping so hard, I ran towards the door. My throat was parched, and my calf muscles burned as I flung the door open. I wanted to cry out for water. I wanted to just lie down outside the door and give in, but instead I stumbled on towards the spot that Iago had chosen. Charlie was already there, with all five of her devices. Gasping and swallowing, I reached her.

'Where's Iago?' I wheezed.

'On his way,' she replied. 'And he's got great news, Renny. He called security, told them what happened. They didn't believe him at first but he showed them the bombs. They've got somewhere we can put the devices. It's bombproof. They use it for testing. They're on their way now. We're probably going to be in trouble, but at least we can stop this.'

My phone rang.

'Sarah,' I wheezed, my lungs still gasping for air.

'Renny, the police - they found Varken's family. Gek had been holding them hostage but they're all fine now.'

'I'm glad,' I answered. 'But what about Gek?'

'I'm sorry, Renny, but he got away,' she answered quietly.

My heart sank. He'd managed to evade us again.

'But I heard from Cam. He and the girls are on their way back here. There was no possibility of retrieving the devices. If Gek goes ahead with this, the European machine will be lost. You need to save that machine, Renny!'

'I understand,' I said, hanging up.

I dropped the devices I'd been holding, gasping as I saw one of the timers. Three minutes! I could make it.

'Where are you going?' screamed Charlie as I raced away.

'There's one left,' I shouted back.

'No, Renny, you'll never make it!

I didn't answer her, just kept on going. I didn't really want to think about that. I had to believe I could do this. But I'm not stupid. I needed a back-up plan. I called my smartest geekfriend.

'Dragosh,' I shouted over the noise of the blood pounding in my ears.

'What is it, Renny?'

'I might need your help. The devices, they're not just EMP bombs. They're real. I mean - they're explosive.'

'Whaaat?'

'We got most of them out and the people here at the facility have a testing chamber we can dump them in.'

'So what's your problem?' he asked.

'One of them wouldn't come loose. I'm going back in to try to get it. But I'm running out of time. I've got less than two minutes...'

'What can I do, Renny?' he asked.

'Try to find a way to hack into their uplink. Just disrupt it somehow. I don't know. Try something...'

My voice was hoarse and croaky.

'OK, I'm on it, Renny, but I can't promise anything.'

'I know, I know, just do your best.'

I raced through the laser building again. I didn't know how much more my legs could take, never mind my heart. I ran forward, my eyes blurring with the sweat that was rolling down my forehead. I thought of Iago and Charlie. At least they'd got their bombs out. At least they were safe!

I flung myself around the corner, not using the wall this time; my arm couldn't take the punishment again. Time began to slow as I felt my coat flying out behind me. *Keep pushing forward, Renny. Don't give up now.*

I was now close enough to see the red lights of the timer. I couldn't read it yet. Just a few more paces.

Now I could see it!

My heart actually stopped beating, or at least I couldn't hear it any more. All sound was swallowed up in a vacuum of space and time. Dust motes flitted through the still air. Nothing changed except the red number on the timer. It counted down from forty-six to forty-five seconds.

I raced to the device and grasped it with both hands. Planting my feet firmly, I leaned back and pulled with all my might. It didn't budge.

I had to act quickly. There had to be something I

could do. *Think, Renny. Think!* Then the science came back to me. I'd been going about this all wrong - trying to use brute force to remove the device. Sometimes the brain is stronger than the body.

I stepped to the right of the device and circled my fingers around the left side of it. This device was held in place by a magnetic seal. If I could interrupt the seal even just slightly then the whole thing should come loose.

With a roar like a lion attacking its prey, I flung myself to the right, my fingers clinging desperately to the left edge.

The device came free so quickly that I was slammed against the blue metal laser housing and the device flew out of my hands.

A screeching noise assaulted my ears as the seconds ticked by. With a shock, I realised that it was my own voice, coming through my open mouth. A final spurt of adrenaline kicked in, and I scrabbled forwards to where the device lay face down on the polished stone floor.

I turned it over in my hands: twenty seconds to go.

I didn't know if I could make it out of the building, but I had to keep hoping. I forced myself onto my feet then staggered back towards the end of the room, my arms flailing, my chest hurting, constantly checking the hideous device in my hand. The seconds ticked down with each step I took. As I glanced up, the end of the blue laser housing looked very far away. Why did this space seem so much bigger now?

As I rounded the corner, I had only ten seconds left. If I could only make it to the door, I could throw the device out. I might not be saved, but the LIFE machine would. Ten seconds to cover fifty metres. Could I do it?

With every ounce of my being, I hurtled forward, head down like a sprinter. All the time my eyes never left the device.

I felt the cool breeze on my cheek as I opened the door. With three seconds left on the timer, I was out in the open space between the buildings. I felt weak with relief. I'd done it! No matter what happened now, the LIFE machine was safe.

My head throbbed and my vision blurred. I looked down at the evil device in my hand. Why was it still there? I could feel my legs wobbling. I just had to throw the device as far away from me as possible. All it would take was one action.

So why couldn't I do it?

I *needed* to get control of my hand.

From somewhere distant, I heard a girl call my name, her voice angelic, soft and sweet. A warm, happy feeling covered me like a blanket. Charlie, everything's going to be fine. I just need to throw this thing away.

I looked down at my hand, but it wasn't mine. At least, it didn't act like mine. It just stayed there, uselessly gripping the device. The red counter continued flashing, but I couldn't make out the numbers. They were upside-down - or backwards - or something...

I closed my eyes. Maybe if I squeezed them hard, they'd work better.

A wave of heat spread across my forehead, and I could see white pinpricks of light behind my eyelids. Then I was floating.

No - not floating.

Falling.

The points of light grew bigger, pushing the darkness aside. I reached out to them. They were so bright and warm and beautiful... they looked like stars.

Stars on Earth.

Everything was white and warm. The machines were safe, and no one had been hurt. Now, after all our adventures, it was time to stop running.

Now I could sleep at last.

Epilogue

Geeknews... newsflash ... Geekboss reported down ... Dragosh - confirm or deny . . .

Dragosh... Geekboss not down ... uplink was disabled ... repeat ... Geekboss is not down ...

He is alive...

Previous **arctic⁶** Adventures

www.arctic6.com